The McKenna Brothers

Three billionaire brothers.
Three guarded hearts. Three fabulous stories.

Meet the gorgeous McKenna Brothers…

In this brand-new trilogy from the wonderfully witty, *New York Times* bestselling author Shirley Jump.

Rich, handsome and successful, they're the most eligible bachelors in Boston!

Find out what happens when the oldest brother, Finn, finds himself propositioned by the intriguing, feisty Ellie Winston in

One Day to Find a Husband
July 2012

Discover whether straight-talking Stace Kettering can tame notorious playboy Riley in

How the Playboy Got Serious
August 2012

Returning hero Brody is back home and has ~~a secret~~… but can he confide in Kate ~~S~~

Return ~~of~~
Se~~~~

D1510067

Dear Reader,

Those McKenna brothers are at it again! I loved writing this series, not just because it's set in the area where I grew up, but because these three brothers and the heroines who challenge them were so much fun. Each brother was a strong, heroic individual, and that gave me unique challenges with each story.

Sometimes, when I create a fictional place like the Morning Glory Diner, it becomes so real to me, I find myself wishing I could go there! I revisit the diner in the last McKenna book (Brody's story) and it was like returning to a favorite place. It was nice to see Heidi the dog again, from Finn's book, and to learn more about the McKenna family matriarch. I hope you enjoy Riley's story and the challenges he faces working with sassy Stace!

I love to hear from readers, too, so please write to me through my website (www.shirleyjump.com) or visit my blog (www.shirleyjump.blogspot.com) where I post family-favorite recipes and writing advice. Share with me your favorite spot to eat, or just your favorite McKenna brother!

Happy reading,

Shirley

SHIRLEY JUMP

How the Playboy Got Serious

HARLEQUIN®

entertain, enrich, inspire™

ISBN-13: 978-0-373-17827-8

HOW THE PLAYBOY GOT SERIOUS

First North American Publication 2012

Copyright © 2012 by Shirley Kawa-Jump, LLC

New York Times bestselling author **Shirley Jump** didn't have the willpower to diet, nor the talent to master under-eye concealer, so she bowed out of a career in television and opted instead for a career where she could be paid to eat at her desk—writing. At first, seeking revenge on her children for their grocery-store tantrums, she sold embarrassing essays about them to anthologies. However, it wasn't enough to feed her growing addiction to writing funny. So she turned to the world of romance novels, where messes are (usually) cleaned up before The End. In the worlds Shirley gets to create and control, the children listen to their parents, the husbands always remember holidays, and the housework is magically done by elves. Though she's thrilled to see her books in stores around the world, Shirley mostly writes because it gives her an excuse to avoid cleaning the toilets and helps feed her shoe habit.

To learn more, visit her website, www.shirleyjump.com.

Books by Shirley Jump

ONE DAY TO FIND A HUSBAND*
THE PRINCESS TEST
HOW TO LASSO A COWBOY
IF THE RED SLIPPER FITS
VEGAS PREGNANCY SURPRISE
BEST MAN SAYS I DO

*The McKenna Brothers trilogy

Other titles by this author available in ebook format.

To my readers. You all are the best part of my job, and I am humbled and honored to write books you enjoy.

CHAPTER ONE

LIFE as Riley McKenna knew it was about to change. And change in a big way. He sensed the change coming, like the shift in the wind when summer yielded to fall.

"I love you, Riley, but I have to say this." Mary McKenna looked her grandson straight in the eye, with the steady light blue gaze that told him she was about to say something he didn't want to hear. "It's high time you grew up."

Gray-haired, elegant and poised, Mary sat in one of two rose-patterned Windsor chairs in what was called the morning room but that Riley and his brothers had long ago dubbed the "serious room," because that was where their grandmother held all her serious talks. When they were young, they knew getting called into the morning room meant a long and stern lecture. Even at twenty-six, Riley was occasionally summoned to this space—and that was exactly what Mary did—summoned—and given the familiar sermon about responsibility and maturity.

Mary had a presence about her, built over years of helming first the family, then the family business. Truth be told, she intimidated most people and even sometimes Riley, because she made no bones about her feelings—ever. So when Mary wanted to have a serious talk, Riley knew enough to listen. But that didn't mean he wasn't going to try to escape the lecture about to come.

"Gran, it's my birthday." He shot her the grin that usually sweet-talked his grandmother into leniency. "That means I'm more grown up today than yesterday."

More or less.

He'd spent the night before his birthday in a bar, and had plans to hit a whole list of them tonight with his friends. He knew he should be looking forward to the night out, but for some reason, the thought of trading the same conversations with the same people over the same beverages sounded...

Boring.

He was just hungover. Or something. He'd be fine once he had a nice dark ale in his hands.

"That is not what I meant, and you know it." Gran sipped a cup of tea while the sun streamed in from the picture window behind her and kissed everything in the stately Victorian style room with gold. The house was over a hundred years old, a towering three-level clothed in dark paneling and the occasional modern touch. Mary could have afforded ten times the house but she had chosen to stay in the place where she had raised her children and loved her husband. To Riley, the house had a certain amount of dependability and comfort, which was half the reason he had yet to move out of the guest house that sat just down the driveway from the main house. He liked being here, liked being surrounded by his DNA's history. And he liked to keep an eye on his grandmother. She had a tendency to do too much, and to rarely listen to anyone who told her otherwise. The McKenna stubborn streak was alive and well in Mary McKenna.

Mary smoothed out a wrinkle that had dared to crimp her plaid skirt. "Your birthday is an occasion to rethink your priorities and focus on more mature pursuits."

More mature pursuits. Which to his grandmother, Riley knew meant getting married. Settling down. Something he avoided at all costs. He glanced out the window and saw a golden fur ball wandering the grounds. His oldest brother's adopted shelter dog, one of the nicest pets Riley had ever met. No wonder Finn spoiled her with treats and toys. "Finn drop his dog off here?"

"I'm watching Heidi for a few days while they take a trip together. She's a wonderful dog." Then Gran leaned forward. "I won't let you change the subject, Riley. This is serious business." She held up a newspaper. "Have you read this morning's *Herald?*"

Uh-oh. "Uh, no."

She laid it down again. "When you do, you will see that you have a starring role in the media. Once again." She sighed. "Really, do we need the world to know every single time you are caught in a compromising position?"

Oh. That. The woman he'd been with that night at the gala had been a little too eager, and he'd been a little too willing. He'd forgotten there'd be reporters skulking about. Before he could say stop, his date had her dress hiked up and her body pressed against his. There'd been a sound behind them, and the entire awkward moment was caught on film. Riley cringed. He hated seeing that look of disappointment on his grandmother's face. He'd let her down. Again. "It was a mistake. I had a little too much to drink—"

"No excuse. You are far past the age where you can act like a fool and get away with it. Your brother has just shipped off to Afghanistan, volunteering, I might add, to help the wounded. And instead of focusing on Brody's charity, the reporter has chosen to make the entire story about you and your…indiscretions." His grandmother leaned closer. "You do realize that you did this at a fundraiser for wounded veterans? The last thing the McKenna Foundation needs is publicity like this. From a family member, no less."

"You're right. It shouldn't have happened." He let out a long breath. "Sometimes I just don't think."

"This isn't the first time, Riley. I love you, but I can't have you smearing the family name." She shook her head. "You get swayed by a pretty smile and a nice pair of legs and forget that you're supposed to be a responsible adult."

Responsible adult. Those were two words no one had ever used to describe Riley. Finn and Brody, yes, but not Riley. Finn, the married CEO, and Brody, a general practice physician now volunteering his skills half a world away. For the hundredth time, Riley felt like he could never measure up to their examples. He excelled in one area—not being excellent.

For a long time that hadn't bothered him at all. He'd always been too busy seeking the next party, the next pretty face, as his grandmother said, to worry what anyone thought of him. But lately…

Well, lately he'd been thinking far too much.

Gran sighed. "I'm getting old—"

"You're decades away from old."

"—and I'm tired of waiting for great grandchildren."

"Finn just gave you one. And they have another on the way already." His oldest brother Finn had taken to marriage like a bear to salmon fishing. Married, one adopted child, and a baby due in a little over seven months. Riley had to admit that sometimes, when he saw how happy Finn and Ellie were, he felt a little...jealous. But only because Finn was so damned happy, it seemed like he'd caught a smiling disease.

"And now it's your turn," Mary said.

"Whoa, whoa. What about Brody? He's next in line for the yoke."

His grandmother pursed her lips at that. "Marriage is not chaining oxen together. Your grandfather and I—"

"Were the exception to the rule. Nobody stays married like that anymore." Even though his grandfather had died a little over three years ago, Mary still carried a torch for the man she had loved for more than five decades. They had been a loving, kind couple, the type that held hands when they rode in the car or walked the neighborhood. When Riley had been young, it had been nice to see, something that made him wonder if he'd ever have a relationship like that. Then he'd grown up, started dating, and realized his grandparents' lifelong love affair was about as common as unicorns in the zoo.

His grandmother took another sip of tea, then laid the china cup into the saucer. "You're just jaded. If you would settle down you might find love is a lot better than you think."

"I'm happy the way I am."

"Perhaps." She toyed with the teaspoon on the tray beside her, then lifted her gaze to her grandson's. Even at seventy-eight, Mary's mind was sharp and agile. She still ran McKenna Media, the advertising company started by her husband. She'd been grumbling about stepping down for years, but had yet to take even a day off. Riley suspected Mary kept working both to stay close to the husband she missed and to keep her days full. "You haven't really done anything with your life yet, Riley."

"I work, Gran."

She scoffed. "You show up at the office, goof off and collect a paycheck."

"Hey, we all have to be good at something. That's my area of expertise."

His grandmother didn't laugh at the joke, or even so much as crack a smile. The mood in the serious room tensed. "I have indulged you far too much because you are the youngest. I always treated you differently, because—" she sighed, and her pale blue eyes softened "—I felt bad for you. Losing your parents at such a young age, then being uprooted from the only home you ever knew to live with your grandfather and I—"

Riley waved that off. "I was fine."

Mary's gaze locked on his. "Were you?"

He looked away, studying the gilt-framed landscape hanging on the far wall. Painted sunlight dappled oil-created trees and brush-formed flowers, and caressed the roofline of a cottage nestled in a fictional forest. A perfect little world, captured in Technicolor paint. "I was fine," Riley repeated.

"I think if you tell yourself that often enough, you'll eventually believe it," Mary said softly.

Riley let out a long breath. He wasn't much for serious talks, or serious conversational topics, or, come to mention it, the serious room. Altogether far too stuffy and formal. And well, hell, *serious.* "I'm supposed to be meeting someone for lunch, Gran." He rose halfway out of the chair. "I really need to get going."

"Cancel your plans."

He cocked a brow. "Oh, now I get it. Are you planning a birthday party for me, Gran? You know you've never been able to surprise me."

"No party this year, Riley. In fact, I think it's high

time your party days were behind you." She steepled her fingers and brought them to her lips. "Sit back down please."

Uh-oh. Riley recognized that stance. It meant Gran had an idea—one he knew he wasn't going to like. He lowered his lanky frame back into the uncomfortable Windsor chair.

"I think you need a real wake-up call, Riley. Consequently—" Gran paused and her pale eyes nailed him like a bug on a board "—I'm cutting you off."

The words hung in the air for a long time before Riley processed them. "You're...what?"

"Effective immediately, you are fired from McKenna Media, not that you had a real job there as it was. And you will also be expected to pay a reasonable rent on the guest house. Every month, on the first. Which happens to be two weeks away."

Gran meant business. No mistaking that.

Riley opened his mouth to argue. To joke. To cajole. To employ any of a dozen techniques he'd used before to talk his stern grandmother out of punishments and edicts.

He didn't. Instead he considered her words and realized she had a point.

Gran had never approved of the way he lived his life. But what his grandmother didn't understand was that Riley didn't spend his days without any sense of commitment because he wanted to shirk responsibilities. It was because he had yet to find a direction that interested him.

He'd tried nearly every job at McKenna Media, and within a few days, been bored to death. He'd dated dozens of beautiful women, but not found a single one who dared his heart to take a risk.

Gran probably wanted Riley to go out and find yet another job in a field he could hardly stand, then settle down with one of her friends' single, available granddaughters. But what Riley really wanted was...

A challenge. Something that made him rush to get out of bed in the morning. Maybe he needed something—God help him—with substance.

Riley had always known this day would come, and for some reason, instead of being panicked by it, he felt...energized. For the first time in a long time.

Had his partying ways finally grown tiresome? No, he told himself. It was a minor bump, a moment of ennui, nothing more. He'd spend a few days doing things his grandmother's way, prove to her that he wasn't nearly as irresponsible as he looked, and then be back to his old life in no time.

"Okay," he said. "I'll do it."

She blinked her surprise. "Well, good." She reached into her pocket and handed him a slip of paper. "Your final paycheck. I'm kicking you out, and cutting you off, but I don't want you to starve the first day."

Riley gave his grandmother a soft smile, then leaned down and brushed a kiss across her wrinkled cheek. "I'll be fine, Gran." He pressed the check back into her hand, then said goodbye and headed out the door, and into a world he had never truly experienced.

He thought it would be easy, like everything else in his life had been.

He was wrong.

Stace Kettering had had enough. "I quit, Frank." She tossed her apron on the counter in emphasis, and slapped her order pad down beside it. The last of the breakfast crowd had left a few minutes earlier, giving Stace her first break since five in the morning. She grabbed a glazed donut out from under the glass dome on the counter and took a bite. "I'm serious. I quit."

Frank let out a laugh. His barrel belly shook with the sound, and his wide smile broke into an even wider grin. Frank Simpson had been the head chef and part owner of Morning Glory Diner for thirty years—almost as long as anyone could remember the burger that had made Frank's famous. Stace had worked there nearly all her life—almost as long as anyone could remember a Kettering offspring at the counter at Frank's.

"I've heard that before," Frank said, emerging from the kitchen to plant his beefy palms on the counter. He gave Stace a wink. "A hundred times. No, maybe two hundred." He picked up her apron and held it out to her.

"I'm serious this time. I'm done." She ignored the apron and took another bite of donut. The sweet glaze melted like heaven on her tongue.

"Is Walter giving you a hard time again? You know he means well."

"He is the grumpiest man in the city of Boston. No, the state of Massachusetts."

Frank chuckled. "I think the entire You-nited States."

That got a laugh out of Stace. "I think you're right." She plopped onto one of the counter stools and let out a sigh. "Why does he always pick my table?"

"He likes you."

Walter was a daily customer at Morning Glory Diner, though Lord only knew why he kept returning when all he did was find fault with everything from the forks to the fries. And every single time, he made sure he was seated in Stace's section, as if he was on a one-man mission to ruin her day. "He told me I was the slowest waitress in the entire solar system, complained that his water was flat—"

"Flat water?" Frank arched a brow. "Did he expect it to be round?"

"I think he ran out of things to complain about." Stace let out another laugh. She put down the donut, then reached for the apron and snatched it back, tugging it over her head before fastening the strings in the back. "Okay, so I won't quit today. But if you don't hire someone else soon, I will quit. On principle." It had been two weeks since Irene had gone on maternity leave, which had left Stace to single-handedly carry the weight of the diners at Frank's until she returned. The tips were great and much needed, but at the end of day, Stace was so tired she needed to be rolled to her little house eight subway stops away. And given the way things had been going at home lately, Stace needed to be alert. There wasn't just her to worry about anymore.

Frank gave her a smile. "You're exhausted, honey."

"I'm okay. Walter just stressed me out, that's all." She eyed the older man. "I'm more worried about how you are. I know business has been down for a while and I hate to see you working so hard."

He wagged a finger at her. "Nope, not falling for that. You know me, if I wasn't fine, I'd be complaining."

She laughed. "Frank, you never complain." Then her gaze softened and her hand covered his. "You keep talking about retiring, but never do. You deserve some time off, Frank."

He waved that off. "If I retire, who's going to make the famous Morning Glory burger?"

"Me."

Frank laughed. "No offense, Stace, but you can't even make grilled cheese. Your dad, God rest his soul, was the same way. Good at the books, good in the front of the house, but a nightmare on the grill." Frank's big brown eyes softened. "I know one thing, though. He'd be awful proud of you."

She glanced around the diner, at the building that her father had built. The morning glory border he had painted himself, the chairs and tables he'd picked out. Every wall in this place still seemed to beat with her father's heart. She missed him, but at least here, she could be close to him, and his memory. For a second, her father's presence filled her heart, surrounded her like a hug. "Thank you, Frank."

He shrugged, then fiddled with a spoon on the counter. "How's things with Jeremy?"

"We're getting there. He's a handful." Handful didn't even begin to describe her nephew, who was angry at his mother, angry at the world...just plain angry. He needed an outlet, something to help him work through the shock of his mother's abandonment, but Stace had yet to find anything the boy would stick with. She bit back a sigh. Later, she'd worry about that. For now, she'd focus on making enough money to handle the additional cost of an extra mouth to feed. While at the same time trying to find a way to increase business at the diner.

"Poor kid's been through a lot," Frank said. "You need anything, you come ask me. I'll be there for you."

Stace's hand covered Frank's beefy palm. The older man had already been a great presence in Jeremy's life, serving as a surrogate grandfather just as he'd served as Stace's surrogate father. Frank had given her a raise she hadn't asked for, quietly dropped off a new TV at her house when hers broke, and taken Jeremy school shopping when he'd refused to go with Stace. Even as she insisted she could handle it herself, Frank stepped in anyway. "I know you will."

Frank's eyes misted, but he let out a cough to cover for the momentary emotion. Frank was a man who loved well and hard, but rarely let that emotion show. Stace had only seen him cry once, and the sight of it had broken her heart because she knew the pain in Frank's heart lanced deep.

Frank cleared his throat. "Anyway, I promise, I'll hire the next person who walks in that door." He pointed toward the diner's glass entrance.

"Right." She laughed. "You've been promising to hire another server for two weeks now, and no one has even gotten past the application stage." Stace pointed at the Help Wanted sign propped in the window. "That thing is doing nothing but gathering dust."

He shrugged. "I'm picky. I can't find enough Stace clones."

"Now you're just buttering me up."

Frank grinned. "Did it work?"

"Yes. But just for today." She swiped the order pad off the counter, and tucked the pen into her pocket. Every time she reached the quitting point, Frank found a way to convince her to stay. Heck, he was right. She'd have stayed with or without the jokes and compliments. Her loyalty to Frank Simpson ran bone-deep, and always would.

"Good." He thumbed the straps of his apron and let out a long breath. "Back to the fryer for me. Those bloomin' onions don't bloom on their own, you know." Just as Frank turned back to the kitchen, the door of the diner opened, causing the overhead bell to let out a soft jangle. The two of them pivoted toward the sound.

Riley McKenna.

If there was a customer Stace dreaded almost as much as Walter, it was Riley. He was a handsome man—if one was the kind of woman who found blue eyes and dark hair appealing. And a charming man—if one liked a man with a ready smile and quick wit. But he was also a playboy, and if there was one thing Stace had no tolerance for, it was playboys.

Even if he took her breath away when he smiled. Damn, he was a good-looking man. Too bad he was all wrong for her.

She'd seen his picture in the papers with the girlfriend of the minute, heard other women talk about him with an actual swoon in their voice. As far as she could tell, the youngest McKenna hadn't followed in the family traditions of meaningful work or charitable organizations. Unless attending every party in the greater Boston area was considered giving back to society.

Stacey avoided men like Riley McKenna like the plague. She'd learned a long time ago that a nice smile and charming words were merely a cover for deeper flaws. Thank God she'd woken up before she married such a man. She'd known Jim for years, and fallen for his charismatic ways over and over again. He'd proposed on a Sunday and left town on a Tuesday—

With a girl he'd met the night before. She'd been fooled for so long, blind to his lies, because she'd wanted to believe in that smile. It had taken her a year to get over the betrayal, and from here on out, Stace would avoid men like that, thank you very much. And that meant avoiding Riley McKenna. And his smile.

Riley nearly always sat in her section and ordered an omelet. Not one of the dozen combinations on the menu, but always something of his own creation, which drove Stace crazy but didn't seem to bother Frank. She knew, from the lackadaisical way he ate his breakfast and the dozens of phone calls she'd overheard where Riley discussed the latest hot party or vacuous date, that his life was about as serious as confetti.

And on top of that, he seemed to think flirting was on the menu. He teased her, smiled at her, and had asked for her number once. Typical. Thinking every woman was just going to fall at his feet.

To her, perpetual flirt Riley McKenna was just another entitled bachelor in a city teeming with them. A man whom she suspected hadn't seen a hard day of work in his life, and never appreciated the hard work of others.

"How are you, Frank?" Riley shot them both a grin, then slid onto one of the counter stools.

"Good, good," Frank said. "And you?"

Riley's smile faltered. "I've had better days."

"Well, if it'll make you feel any better, I've got apple pie on the menu today," Frank said.

"Not today, thanks. Unless you're giving out free samples. I'm, ah, currently between funds right now."

"You?" Frank asked. "What, did you spend too much on a date last night?"

"Something like that." Riley gave Frank the cocky grin he gave everyone. The grin that said he'd probably spent his night bedding yet another in a long string of blondes. Stace kept on working. And ignoring him.

Stace soaked a cloth in disinfectant cleaner then started wiping down the pale yellow laminate counter. There wasn't much time before the lunch crowd began to filter in, and lots to do.

"I've been out looking for a job," Riley said.

"I take it the job search hasn't gone too well?"

Riley's grin raised a little on one side. "I'm not qualified to do much."

Frank laughed. Stace restrained herself from issuing a hearty agreement. "I'm sure you'll find something that works for you," Frank said.

"Actually…" Riley began.

Something white caught Stace's eye and she raised her gaze to see what it was. She froze.

"I thought I'd apply here," Riley said. He lifted the Help Wanted sign in his hands, the same one that had been in the window just moments before, and gave Frank a smile. "I figure I eat here enough, I might as well earn my keep."

Frank arched a brow. "You want to be a waiter? Here?"

"Yup. Consider this my official application." Riley slid the sign across the counter.

Frank sent Stace a glance. She mouthed "no," and waved her hands. Frank wouldn't dare. He'd said he'd hire someone, but surely he wanted someone with experience, someone who would be a help, not a hindrance. Someone who had a good work ethic. "Frank…"

Frank grinned at her word of caution, then turned back to Riley. "I told Miss Stace here that I'd hire the next person who walked through that door—"

He wouldn't.

"And since I'm a man of my word—"

He couldn't.

"You're hired, Riley McKenna." Frank reached over and clapped Riley on the shoulder. "Welcome to Morning Glory Diner. Stace here will be glad to show you the ropes."

He did.

Stace plastered a smile she didn't feel on her face, and faced her worst nightmare. An irresponsible womanizer who was going to make her life a living hell.

CHAPTER TWO

ONE day, two tops, Riley figured, and his grandmother would call him back to McKenna Media. Riley could have called in a favor with a friend, but that wouldn't prove he could do anything other than pick up the phone. Sure, waiting tables wasn't the ideal job, but it would do for now, and prove his point to his grandmother that he wasn't the irresponsible man she thought him to be. He looked around the bustling diner. He'd wanted a challenge, something a little different.

And this fit the bill to a T.

So Riley donned the black apron imprinted with Morning Glory Diner on the pocket, grabbed an order pad and pen, and crossed to the first set of customers he saw. Before he could even open his mouth, that waitress—Sally, Sandy—rushed over and nearly tackled him. "You can't take this table."

"I'm doing it. Watch me take their order, too." He clicked the pen, and faced the two construction workers whose broad frames nearly filled either side of the booth. Beefy guys in dusty T-shirts and jeans. "What can I get you guys?"

The first one, a nearly bald fiftyish man wearing a bright yellow hat emblazoned with Irving in thick black marker, gave Riley an are-you-an-idiot look. "Menus."

Riley glanced down and realized he had forgotten that important first step. No problem. He'd get it right the next time. This was waiting tables; it wasn't rocket science. "Right. Those would be helpful. Unless you just want to make up an order, and I'll zip it back to Frank in the kitchen." Riley thumbed toward the kitchen.

Sally/Sandy smacked his arm. "You can't just make up food. I've told you that a hundred times." Then she turned to the two men. "I apologize. He's new. Probably won't last long. Let me get you some menus." She turned on her sneakered heel, and started to walk away, then thought better of it, and grabbed a fistful of Riley's shirt and hauled him backward.

Riley's feet tangled and nearly brought him to the ground. "Hey, hey, hey! What are you doing?"

"Getting you out of there before you do any more damage." She stopped by the hostess station, snatched up two menus, then released Riley. "Stay." She punctuated the word with a glare. "And I mean it."

"Woof."

The glare intensified, then she stalked off, handed the menus to the customers, and returned to Riley's side. "Hey, all I did was forget menus. You're acting like I committed a federal crime," he said.

"Just stay out of my way and we'll get along just fine."

"I'm supposed to be making your life easier."

"Well, you're not."

She started to walk away, but he caught up with her and turned her to face him. "I was hired to help you."

"Well, you're not."

He eyed Sally/Sandy. He'd had the pretty blonde as a waitress a dozen times, and though he'd tried his best to get to know her, she'd resisted. Maybe she hated him. Why?

Maybe because he'd never learned her name, something he now regretted. And couldn't remedy because she didn't have on a name tag.

She was a beautiful woman with a petite, tight body and a smile that rarely made an appearance. She had wide green eyes, long blond hair that he'd only ever seen tied back, and a quick wit. He'd seen her friendly banter with other customers, and wondered why she'd always been cold with him on the dozens of occasions when he'd eaten here.

He'd asked her out a few times, flirted with her often, and she'd always resisted. Now he needed to get along with her—at least on the job. Ordinarily, he wouldn't care—he'd just avoid her at work or just avoid work, period. But this time, the job mattered, not just because he needed the paycheck, but because he wanted to prove himself, to Gran, to himself, and yes, in an odd way, to this angry waitress. "I admit, I have no idea what the hell I'm doing here," he said. "I'm on a steep learning curve, and that means I might get underfoot a little."

"A lot," she corrected.

"Okay, a lot. But I'm here to help, to take some of the burden off your shoulders. If you let me."

She let out a sigh. "What am I going to do with you?"

"Train me." He put up his two hands. "I can sit, stay and even beg."

"Just…stay," she said now. "You're no good to me out there. You'll just make my job harder."

"Why? You think I can't write down an order and deliver it to Frank?" He'd seen her do it a hundred times. It didn't look hard at all.

"Honestly, no."

"Why not?"

"Because a man with manicured nails and a thousand-dollar haircut is used to giving orders, not taking them."

Riley winced. Did people really see him that way? A useless playboy with nothing but time on his hands for mischief? And if they did, could he blame them? What had he done with his life up until now? But he was determined to change that, at least here, now, in this diner. "Frank hired me for a reason."

"Because he promised me he'd hire the next person who walked through that door. It could have been a monkey, and Frank would have given him a job just to prove his point."

"Which is?"

She let out a gust. "What do you care? You're only here because you needed something else to amuse you." The bell over the door jangled, and two more customers stepped inside the diner. She grabbed some menus out of the bin by the hostess station. "I don't want to be part of your little 'live like the common folk do' project." She put air quotes around the words.

"I'm not—"

But she was already gone, seeming to whoosh across the tiled floor like a tidal wave. In the space of thirty seconds, she had the second couple seated, given them their menus, then returned to the construction workers and taken their orders. She tore a page off the pad, slipped behind the counter and slid it across the stainless steel bar in the kitchen to Frank, calling off something Riley couldn't understand but sounded like "flop two, over easy" and "give it wings."

Frank garbled something back, and Sally/Sandy disappeared into the kitchen for a second.

Riley had to admit, he was impressed. He had watched her bustle around the diner, a tiny dynamo in a slim fitting pair of jeans, a hot pink Morning Glory Diner T-shirt, and a bobbing blond ponytail. Every time he'd seen her, she'd been like that, a human bee, flitting from one table to the next. She was fast, and efficient, even if her customer service skills with him were almost nonexistent. Maybe the job was more stressful than it looked. Many times, she'd been the only waitress in here when he stopped in for his morning breakfast, since lunch was almost always at McGill's Pub with his brother Finn.

Apparently help was hard to come by, because he'd seen that Help Wanted sign often over the years, and seen dozens of waitresses who worked here a few weeks, then moved on. The only constant was Sally/Sandy—he was sure it was something with an *S*—she had been here every day, and always with the same brisk, no-nonsense approach to the job.

"Hey, buddy, you just going to stand there?"

Riley leaned against the hostess station, flipping through one of the menus. He'd been given the menu before, but never really looked at it. He'd just ordered what he wanted and figured if they didn't have the ingredients, they would have told him. Now, though, it might be a good idea to get more familiar with it. Knowing Sally/Sandy, there'd be a quiz later.

"Buddy!"

Frank's offered a hell of a lot of food for such a small place. He'd started coming here in the mornings for breakfast because it was on the way between his subway stop and the offices of McKenna Media. Not to mention the Morning Glory's coffee was better than any he'd ever had. Riley scanned the pages of breakfast and lunch offerings, noted there was no dinner service. Working half days sounded good to him. He'd have his evenings free.

Except, the thought of spending an evening in yet another bar didn't thrill him anymore. Maybe it was being another year older. Maybe it was the shock of Gran's edict. Maybe it was a need for new friends. Whatever the problem was, he knew one thing.

He wanted more…depth to his days.

"Hey, moron!"

Riley jerked his attention toward the construction guys. "You can't talk to her like that."

"Her who? We're talking to you, Tweedledee." The two guys snickered, then the big one—the one with the hat that said Irving—wiggled his fingers like he was feigning sign language. "Two coffees. You know, the hot stuff in cups?"

"I know what coffee is."

"Good. Get us some. *Now.*"

Bunch of Neanderthals ordering people around. Riley leaned against the hostess station and crossed his arms over his chest. Considered dumping the pot in the man's lap, just to prove the point. "No. Not unless you say please."

Irving's face turned red. His fist tightened on the table. Before he could open his mouth, Sally/Sandy came sailing past Riley, two cups in one hand, a hot pot of coffee in the other. The cups landed on the table with a soft clatter, and she filled them to just under the brim without spilling a drop. "Don't mind him. He's not really a waiter."

"What is he?" Irving said.

"I think you already called it. What was the word?" She put a finger to her lips. "Oh yes, moron."

The two men laughed some more at that. They thanked her, then sat back and started talking about work.

The waitress had an ease with smoothing the customers' ruffled feathers. He'd noticed that about her before—she'd turned more than one disgruntled frown into a smile. It was what had interested him about her before, and still did now. She was a contradiction. And that intrigued him. A lot.

Sally/Sandy returned, grabbed Riley's shirt again and tugged him around to the other side of the counter. She was surprisingly strong for such a petite woman.

"Hey, go easy on the manhandling," Riley said and gently disengaged her hand.

She snorted. "Manhandling. Right."

He leaned against the counter and eyed her. "Why do you hate me so much?"

"I don't hate you. You annoy me. There's a difference." He opened his mouth to ask a question but she put a hand up and stopped him. "Listen, I'd love to talk all day about your faults—"

"I don't have any faults." He grinned. "Okay, maybe one."

"But the lunch crowd will be here any second, and I have work to do."

"So do I. Are you going to let me do my job?"

"You can't handle this job."

"Let me prove it to you." He took a step closer. Wow, she had pretty eyes. They were the color of emeralds, a deep, dark green that seemed to beckon him in. "Listen, I've watched you work, and if you ask me, you work too hard."

"This job demands hard work."

"Not if you have readily available help to call on.

Something I've never seen you do, even when the other woman was working here. I can be useful, you know."

She let out a long breath, and Riley found himself wondering what was in that breath that she wasn't saying. What weights sat on her delicate shoulders. "I just feel better doing things myself."

"Asking for help doesn't make you weak. Just smart."

She cocked a brow. "And asking for *your* help, what does that make me?"

"Brilliant." He grinned.

She eyed him for a long, long time, while the coffee-pot percolated and the hum of conversation filled the air. "All right, I'll be better about letting you help. But stay out of my way and don't screw up. Don't flirt with the customers, and don't flirt with me. Just keep your head down and work." She narrowed her gaze at him. "Because when you screw up, it costs me, and I can't afford to let that happen. Got it?"

"Got it, captain." He gave her a mock salute.

She scowled. "And don't call me captain."

He leaned in, gave her another grin. "What should I call you?"

She held his gaze for a long moment. "Stace would be fine."

Stace. He liked that name. A short, no-nonsense name seemed to suit her.

"And you can call me Riley," he said, putting out his hand to shake hers. "I like it a whole lot better than moron."

Riley McKenna. The man had clearly been put on this earth—and in this diner—to drive her nuts. Stace had to stay on top of him for the entire lunch wave, which only complicated her job. He couldn't take an order, couldn't remember the menus, didn't know where anything was, and delivered the wrong food to the wrong table five times.

Not to mention he moved like a turtle on Valium.

He'd told her to let him help her, and she now regretted agreeing.

Worst of all, he kept attracting her attention. Tall, dark-haired, blue-eyed, the kind of guy that wore a smile like it was cologne. He had on dark wash jeans and a golf shirt, with boat shoes, even though she doubted he had been heading for a boat today. She had to force herself more than once to concentrate on her job, instead of on him.

When the lunch demand eased, Stace slipped into the kitchen. "What were you thinking?" she said.

Frank put a finger to his temples. "Uh, that my salsa dancing days are behind me, but I can still cut a mean foxtrot."

She laughed. "You are a pain in my butt."

"I know, and you love me for it." Frank grinned, then wrapped an arm around Stace's shoulders.

She leaned into his embrace. Frank's thick arms and broad chest enveloped her like a teddy bear. She'd known Frank all her life, and even though he'd told her a thousand times that she could get a better job than waitressing for him, she stayed. Not because she loved waitressing so much, but because she loved Frank and loved the Morning Glory. Frank hadn't just been her father's best friend, he'd been her father, too, in every way but biology, and she couldn't imagine not seeing his familiar craggy face every day. Or this diner, which held so many of Stace's memories in this one small building. "Thanks for keeping me sane, Frank."

"Anytime." His voice was gruff. He turned to the

sink to wash his hands before he got back to work slicing tomatoes. "How's the new guy working out?"

"Terrible. He can't take orders, can't deliver food to the right tables, can't pour coffee without scalding someone."

Frank chuckled. "He'll learn."

"Why on earth would you hire him? He has no experience, no customer service skills and no—"

"Job. The guy needed a job." Frank shrugged. "So I gave him one."

Stace eyed her boss and friend. "You don't take pity on people like that. You're usually harder on the staff than I am. What's up?"

Frank paused and put the knife down. The blade seemed small next to his beefy palms. "Riley's been coming in here for a long time."

"Years."

"And he's been a bit of a pain."

"A bit? The man is an incorrigible flirt. And he's always asking for some custom thing or another."

"But at heart, he's a good guy."

"How do you know that?"

Frank considered her for a moment. "I just know. I'll let you figure that out for yourself. You'll see what I see."

She snorted. "I doubt it."

"Just have an open heart," Frank said. "You're a sweet girl, Stace, but your heart is closed off. Hell, you have a big old detour sign outside it."

"I have reasons why," she said softly.

"Don't you think it's past time you opened that road again?"

She glanced out the window, at the busy city that had once seemed to hold such promise, but then one day had stolen her biggest dream, and shook her head. Some days, being at the Morning Glory was so painful, she wasn't sure she could stay another minute. Other days, she couldn't imagine ever leaving. "Not now."

Maybe not ever.

She had her priorities now—a nephew who had been abandoned by his mother—and that meant she didn't have time or need for a relationship. It wasn't about not wanting to take that risk again—

Okay, maybe it was.

Either way, she didn't have time. Or room for a handsome, distracting man.

She pivoted toward the counter, took the two BLTs Frank had finished assembling, and hurried out of the kitchen, before the man who knew her better than anyone in the world could read the truth in her eyes.

That Stace wasn't so sure she had enough heart left to ever risk it again.

CHAPTER THREE

THIRTY minutes into the lunch rush, things fell apart. Riley had gone into the whole waiter job with a cocky, self-assured attitude, thinking this job, while busy, was relatively straightforward. Not easy, not once there was more than one table to juggle, but at least relatively manageable. More or less.

Then he'd been assigned Table Seven.

Stace had left him to his own devices. She'd hovered over him for the first couple of tables, but then the diner filled with customers, and she'd been too busy to supervise. "If you need something, don't be stubborn. Ask me," she'd said.

"I did. You turned me down."

She let out a gust. "Get your own orders, your own coffees. I'm not your personal servant."

He had asked her a few times to retrieve things for him. He'd thought she wanted to help him, not throw him into shark-infested waters without so much as a lifejacket. "I didn't—"

"You did. Treat this like a real job and we'll get along a whole lot better. And most of all, don't be an idiot."

He grinned at her. "You like me. Admit it."

"I despise you. Face it." But a smile played on her lips for a split second, before she spun on her heel and headed over to take care of two couples that came in and sat at one of the square tables. A four-top or something, she'd called it.

He watched her go, wondering why he cared that this one woman liked him. Riley McKenna had dated a lot of women. Proposed a few times, then found a way to wriggle out of the impulsive question. Though he entertained the idea from time to time, at his core, he wasn't much for settling down. He'd seen the American Dream at play in only a handful of the people in his life, and to Riley, that meant the odds that he could have the same were between slim and none.

Boston was an ocean with a whole lot of female fish to choose from, and yet, he found himself trying to make Stace smile. Trying to catch her eye. Trying to impress her with his skills. And failing miserably. He'd watched the diner's activity rise and fall, along with her irritation level, and wondered if perhaps the low income generated by the inexpensive food had her stressed.

He'd noticed the place struggling over the last few months, caught in the same bad economy as so many other businesses. What the diner needed was a new marketing approach, one that would give it some attention in Boston's crowded food industry. Riley pondered that as he crossed to Table Seven, another four-top, as Stace called it, which sat in the corner by the window. For whatever reason, Stace had seated this lone man at a table for four.

Before Riley said a word, the man put up a hand. He was tall, thin, with a thick graying beard that made him look like a human grizzly, a fact augmented by the thick dark brown plaid flannel shirt and the cargo pants he wore. For some reason, he looked familiar to Riley, but Riley couldn't place the face.

"You're new," the man said, "so I'm going to do this quick. I don't want a menu. I don't want advice, and I sure as hell don't want your opinion about the special of the day. I want a hot cup of coffee—hot, not luke-warm, not mildly hot, but *hot*—and a cheeseburger with fries. Don't skimp on the fries and don't eat any in the kitchen."

"I wouldn't—"

The man ignored Riley and barreled forward. "The cheeseburger better be well done. That means cooked through. Not so much as a hint of pink. Done, dead, and dark. You hear me? I don't need E. coli as a side dish."

Riley jotted down *burger, fries and coffee* on his pad. Wrote *well done* and underlined it three times. "Right away, sir."

"Don't call me sir or buddy or pal. I don't need a new friend. All I want is my damned food." The man eyed Riley up and down. "What the hell was Frank thinking when he hired you? You look about as much like a waiter as a walrus."

Riley started to answer. The man put up his hand again. "I don't need an answer. I'm not interested in your sob story. It'll be the same as every other one I've heard. Lost my job, lost my apartment, lost my damned dog. I don't care. Just get my food." Then the man shook out his newspaper and buried his nose in the Sports section.

Riley turned away and headed for the kitchen. Before he could give Frank the order, the older man was laughing. "I see you met Walter," Frank said.

"If you're talking about Table Seven, yes." Riley ran a hand through his hair. "Is he always that pleasant?"

"Today he's in a good mood. Usually he yells his order at me from across the room." Frank plopped a fat burger onto the griddle, then turned to drop some fries into a fry basket. "You better go get his coffee. Walter doesn't like to be kept waiting."

On the way to the coffee, Riley got sidetracked by a customer who had to get to a meeting and wanted his order to go. Another who asked to add a salad to his lunch order and a third who wanted extra napkins. Riley dashed from place to place, trying to keep everyone happy, and wondering how Stace—who had twice the number of tables—managed to make it look so easy and he managed to feel like he was coming up short again and again. What he needed was an assistant, something he knew Stace sure as hell wouldn't approve. Hell, he'd had two assistants at McKenna Media. Now…none.

He wasn't used to being the gofer. Or the go-to anything. Riley had never expected the job to be this time-consuming or difficult. Yet Stace made it look effortless. She greeted every customer with a smile, seemed to sail from kitchen to table, and never missed a step. He caught himself watching her, more than once.

"New guy! Coffee!"

Riley jerked to attention and waved at Walter, then turned to the coffeepot and poured a hot cup of coffee. Just as he turned to bring over the mug, Frank dinged the kitchen bell. "Order up. Table Seven."

Riley pivoted back, grabbed the plate, and headed for Walter at a fast clip. The plate jiggled a little as he navigated the crowded diner, but he recovered his balance and delivered the lunch to Table Seven. "Here you go. One burger well done, side of fries, coffee."

Walter gave the entire thing a look of distaste. "I said hot coffee. This isn't hot."

"It's fresh out—"

"You poured it, then went to the kitchen. I don't care if it took you three seconds or thirty, my coffee is cooling while you dawdle and drool over your coworker. And as for my burger and fries—" he lifted the bun, grunted apparent approval at the charred beef, then ran a finger over the fries "—there are only twenty-one fries here. My order comes with twenty-two. No more, no less. I paid for twenty-two. I want that fry."

Across the room, Stace watched the exchange with a slight grin playing on her lips. She was clearly enjoying this.

"I'll get right back to the kitchen," Riley said, "and—"

"Start over. Bring me the whole thing again. From the top. Twenty-two fries."

"Sir, I can bring you more fries—"

"I don't want more fries, I want the ones I ordered." Walter leaned forward. "Did you eat it?"

Riley could swear he heard Stace let out a snicker.

"No, no. I would never—"

"You smell like fries. You ate my fry."

Out of the corner of his eye, Riley noticed a long pale rectangle on the floor. The missing fry, probably had taken a tumble when Riley had dodged a customer shoving back in his chair. "Sir—" A light, quick touch on his arm cut off Riley's words.

"Walter, you don't need to be giving the new guy such a hard time." Stace flipped out a coffee mug, and filled it with hot coffee. "Why, you'll scare him away before he finishes his first day."

Walter took a sip of the coffee. Something that approached a smile flitted across his lips. "Why'd you dump him on my table?"

"Because you're my best customer, that's why." Stace gave Walter a friendly look. "Now let me get you some new fries. And an extra pickle for your troubles."

Walter weighed the offer. "All right. But tell him—" he thumbed in Riley's direction "—to get his head out from between his—"

"Don't say mean things, Walter. It gives you indigestion." She flashed another smile, then turned on her heel and headed for the kitchen.

Riley caught up with her just inside the double doors. The movement brought them close together in the small space, so close, he could catch the vanilla and floral notes of her perfume. It danced around his senses. Sweet, light, enticing. "How'd you get Sir Surly there to smile like that?"

"Easy. I just feed into Walter's need to be right. And his addiction to pickles. Walter can be a pain in the butt—" she arched a brow in Riley's direction, and he wondered if that was a side reference to himself "—but he's all right. He just likes things the way he likes them."

He grinned. "Remind you of anyone you know?"

"Not at all." Stace blew on her nails and feigned indifference. That same slight smile teased at her lips again. "Why? Are you volunteering?"

Riley liked her. He always had. It had to be the way she stood up to him, and gave back as good as she got. She didn't fawn over him or gush compliments like a leaky faucet. She was straight, no-nonsense, what you see is what you get and if you don't like it, too bad.

And he liked that.

"Not at all," he said. A glint of devilish mischief danced in her green eyes, toyed with the corners of her smile. Maybe his being here had reduced the stress on her shoulders. "You gave me that table on purpose."

Stace turned and called back to the kitchen. "Frank, I need another order of fries."

He leaned around until she was looking at him again. "You know, and I know, that you set me up."

The grin playing at the corners of her lips rose a little higher. "Maybe."

"Part of the whole 'make the new guy's life miserable and maybe he'll quit' approach?"

She laughed. When she did, her features lit up, her eyes danced even more. "Did it work?"

"Not a chance." He took the fresh basket of fries from Frank's hands, then headed out the double doors. "You're stuck with me for a while."

"Don't bet on it," she called after him.

Riley was sure he heard Stace laughing as the door swung shut. Mission One accomplished. And it felt better than he'd thought.

He'd made dozens of women smile before, but never had it seemed like such a victory. And never had he worked so hard, nor cared so much about whether someone liked him. He was here for a job, nothing more, and getting distracted by the pretty and sassy waitress across the room would be a mistake.

Hadn't he learned that lesson already? When he let a beautiful face send him off course, it ended up in a disaster. And very often, that disaster made it into the papers. If he was going to do this, he was going to do it without dating his coworker.

An hour later, the lunch crowd had left, and the diner was empty. Frank stayed in the kitchen, cleaning up from that day and prepping for the next. Stace flipped the diner's sign to Closed, then turned the lock on the door.

Riley glanced at his watch. Just past three in the afternoon. He could probably catch up to his cousin Alec, and a few of his friends, see what they had cooking.

Alec, a day trader, often started his nights in the afternoon. Time spent with Alec was always memorable, if not a little beer-filled. Riley didn't have his usual budget to spend tonight, but he could make do with the tips in his pocket.

Riley headed to the back of the diner, pulled out his cell, dialed Alec's number and got the rundown on the evening's plans. As his cousin talked about the view from the bar, Riley glanced across the room at Stace, who was emptying the coffeepot. Even with her hair back in a ponytail and wearing an apron and jeans, she was beautiful. "Where I'm at has a pretty good view, too," Riley said. Alec started to make a joke, but Riley cut him off. "Hey, I gotta go. I'll catch up with you later."

He lingered a while longer in the back of the diner. Stace, unaware of him, had turned on the radio and was singing along. She had a light, lyrical voice, and she paused a moment to do a twirl, and toss a discarded napkin into the trash. For a moment, she looked…happy.

He crossed the room. Where did Stace go when her day was over? Why did she work in this diner when she seemed smart enough and determined enough to handle any job? And what would it take to make her smile like she was right now?

She jerked to a stop when she saw him. "Riley. Did you need something?"

He undid the apron, then draped it over one of the chairs. "I'm heading out." He almost said "home" then remembered Gran was charging him rent, a rent he'd only made a minuscule dent in paying, given the paltry tips in his pocket. He could have moved in with one of his brothers, but Finn was out of town and Brody was in Afghanistan. Riley could lean on one of his friends, but as he ran through a mental list, he realized there was no one he was close enough to to impinge on as a roommate.

What did that say about his life? That he didn't have one best friend to call during an emergency?

Riley shrugged off the thought. He'd figure it out, and he'd come out on top. He always did. "See you tomorrow."

"You can't leave yet," Stace said. "We still have to clean up."

He glanced around the diner. Most of the dishes had been cleared away, and the chairs sat square against the tables. "Looks clean to me."

"Right." Stace laughed, then slapped a rag into his hands. "I'll get the salt and pepper shakers off the table and you wipe. If we work together, we'll be out of here faster. Then we can argue over who mops the floor."

Wipe tables? Mop the floors? What was she going to have him do next, clean the windows? "Don't you pay someone to come in and do that stuff?"

She laughed. "Yeah. You. And me."

"Do you ever sit down?" he asked.

She laughed again. Damn, he liked her laugh. "If I do, then I'll fall asleep."

Her mood was lighter, and he liked that. It made the whole diner seem...sunnier. Still, the busy hours he had worked already had him dragging. The thought of staying longer—to clean, something Riley hadn't done since he was a kid and sentenced to kitchen duty for breaking the rules—made him feel even more exhausted.

He'd much rather be sitting in Flanagan's with Alec and Bill, knocking back a few.

"Sorry." He put the wet rag into her hands. "I have plans."

"No, you have a job. And that means you do what needs to be done. You don't just sponge it off on someone else."

He started to disagree. Then realized he'd been doing exactly that.

She pointed at the nearest table, then dangled the rag over his hand. "So get to work."

He leaned in close, searching her emerald gaze with his own. "Is this what you are, Stace? All work and no play? You don't ever blow off work?"

"No, I don't. Because I have priorities. And right now my priority is getting this diner clean so I can go home."

"Why?"

"What do you mean, why?"

"Why this place? It's just a diner."

"It's not just a diner. It's…special. And this job might be hard, but in the end, it's worth it. It's all worth it." Her gaze lit on the tables, the walls, the menus, then she shook her head, and the moment of vulnerability he had glimpsed disappeared. "Anyway, I have work to do."

She crossed to the table, and started clearing the last of the dishes, loading them into a big plastic tub nearby. A hit from the seventies played on the sound system, and Stace began to hum along, her hips swaying gently back and forth as she worked.

He thought of the guys, waiting for him down the street. There, they had beer and women, and—

And the same thing he had done every night for the past six years. He'd been there, done that, as the saying went, and wanted something else. What that something was, he didn't know, but maybe if he stayed here a little while longer with this woman who hummed while she worked a tough job, he'd figure it out.

* * *

After the third day, Stace had to give Riley some credit. Not a lot, and not easily, but she did. The playboy, who from what she'd seen and heard, had never seemed to be much good at anything other than goofing off, had put in several hours at the diner and stayed to clean up afterward. They'd been through a half-dozen waitresses in the past year, and few stayed after tangling with Walter, or getting Frank on a bad day.

But Riley, the last person in the world she would have picked, had stayed. Why? If this job was just a lark—the well-off spending a day in the shoes of the other half—then why was he still here? Did he really need the money?

What she'd heard and read of the McKennas suggested they weren't hurting in the cash department. Then why was the youngest McKenna hoofing it at a diner?

And why did she care? She didn't need a man in her life. She barely had enough room for herself.

Still, she liked that he had put in the hours, and she had to admit, she was beginning to like him. Look forward to seeing him. And his damnable smile. Even as she told herself to steer clear of his charm.

After working together for a few days, they'd worked out a system of partnership. They had cleaned half the tables already, and stacked the chairs to ready the floor for mopping—a big job, after two solid days of rain and muddy footprints. Frank was still in the kitchen, taking care of the dishes and next day's prep. Stace had offered to help, but stubborn Frank had insisted on doing the job himself. For a long time, he'd had a couple of helpers in the kitchen, but since the business had taken a downturn, he'd taken the entire kitchen load on his own shoulders. She sighed.

Frank had talked about traveling the world a hundred times, but never taken a step toward his dream. His health had been poor, something she was sure the stress of the diner augmented, and that just increased her determination to save her pennies and buy out Frank, something she'd offered a hundred times to do, and always he'd said no.

Maybe if she could increase sales he'd be able to hire back some help, and afford some time off. Either way, it wasn't something she could change today.

Stace paused to stretch her back and work out some of the kinks. She bent her neck right, left, then let out a deep breath.

"Tired?" Riley asked.

"Always." She tried to smile, but even that was too much right now. The day had been long, and had a long way to go yet. Jeremy would be leaving school soon and that meant her second shift as temporary mom to a difficult teenager was about to start. Frank had increased the volume on the radio, and his favorite oldies pulsed in the bright space. She cringed at the memory of Riley catching her in that unguarded moment a couple of days ago.

Riley studied her for so long she finally looked away, pretending that she was inspecting the diner. Why did his mere presence affect her so?

"Why don't you take a load off?" he said. "I'll get the rest of this."

"I really should—"

He jerked out a chair and waved toward the seat. "You really should sit, and let me help you."

"Why?"

"Because you're tired." He took the rag out of her hands, before she could protest. "And because I'm not nearly as bad as you think I am."

Exhaustion finally won the battle, and Stace dropped into the chair. "Just for a minute."

Riley grinned. "Take as many minutes as you need."

In fast, efficient movements, he tackled the rest of the tables. He removed all the salt and pepper shakers, then the sugar dispensers, before wiping them in quick but thorough circles. He'd paid attention to her instructions, clearly. Her respect for him inched upward another notch. Still, the pampered marketing exec didn't belong here, and she wondered for the hundredth time why he had taken the job.

"Tell me something," she said.

"What?"

"Why are you here?"

"I work here. Remember?" He flashed that grin at her again. The man smiled a lot, that was for sure. And if she'd been the kind of woman looking for a man who smiled like that, well, she'd be…tempted.

But she wasn't. Not one bit. Uh-uh.

"I know that. I meant why did you get a job here, as a waiter? Don't you work at an ad agency or something?"

"I used to. I got…fired. Sort of."

"How does someone get sort of fired?"

"I worked for my grandmother. She thought it was time I found other employment." He finished the last table, sent the rag sailing toward the bucket of dirty dishes, and waited for it to land with a satisfying thud before he returned to where Stace was sitting. He spun the opposite chair around and sat, draping his arms over the back. "She gets these ideas sometimes, and this was her latest."

"Ideas? On what?"

"On what's good for the McKenna boys." Riley chuckled and shook his head.

Stace's curiosity piqued. She told herself she didn't need to know anything more about this man than whether he would show up tomorrow. She knew his type. Knew better than to fall for a smile and a flirt. But that didn't stop the questions from spilling out of her mouth. "And what *is* good for the McKenna boys?"

"Hard work, beautiful women, and a good Irish stout."

She laughed. "Beer? Your grandmother really said that?"

"I might have added that one." Another grin. But Riley didn't expound on much more than that, and she realized even after three days, she knew little about him.

"And you have, what, two out of the three?" she asked.

"Right now, I have none. Unless Frank keeps some good, dark beer back there."

"No, definitely not."

"Then I'm batting a thousand."

"I don't know about that," she said. "You got the hard work over the last few days."

"True." He leaned forward, his blue eyes zeroing in on her features. "What about you? Why are you working here?"

She looked away. "It's my job."

"I know that," he said, repeating her words from before. "But what I want to know is why. You're smart and efficient. You could do a hundred things other than waitress."

She bristled and got to her feet. "We have a floor to clean. I can't sit around all day."

"Sorry." Riley rose, too. "I shouldn't have probed. I don't like people poking around in my private life. I shouldn't do it to you."

"Remember that, and we might just be able to work together."

It was her way of warning him off. She didn't want to get close to him, or to any man, right now. She had her priorities—working hard, saving money, and raising Jeremy—and there was no room in her life for a man like Riley, who'd just drain her heart and leave her empty in the end.

His gaze took in the glistening tables, the stacked chairs. "We did pretty good today."

"We did. Thanks for the help, and the rest. I needed it." She tossed him his apron. "I'll see you at five, playboy. And that's a.m., not p.m., so don't have too much of number three tonight."

"I was here at five this morning."

"No, you were here at five-fifteen today. Five-thirty yesterday." She worked another kink out of her neck. "That means I have to pick up the slack."

"Getting up early isn't exactly my strong suit." He made an apologetic face.

"You'll learn."

"Learn what?"

She shifted the chair until it was square against the table. "That you can't have it all, Riley."

He moved closer. "Speaking from experience?"

She turned away. "Just giving you friendly advice."

"Are you saying you never go out after work? There's no special guy who takes you out on the town?"

"I'm saying that I keep my life list in order," she said, turning back to him. "And my list is definitely different from—" The diner's door opened and Jeremy burst in the room. She could tell before her nephew even opened his mouth that bad news was coming.

"I'm never going back to that school again," Jeremy said. "It sucks. My whole life sucks."

Stace ached to put an arm around her nephew, to hug him, but she could see him already pulling back. The last year had been hard on him and whenever anyone got too close, he backed up. Years ago, her nephew had told her everything, come to her whenever he was upset. But lately…he'd been as distant as a man on the moon. "Jer, whatever happened today will be better tomorrow. I promise."

Jeremy snorted, then dumped his backpack on the floor. His mane of dark hair hung halfway over his face, obscuring his wide brown eyes from view. "I doubt that. Because I got expelled."

"Are you serious?" Stace's breath left her in a whoosh. "How? Why?"

He shrugged. "The stupid principal thought the drawing I hung in the hall was 'inappropriate.'" He waved air quotes around the word. "Whatever. I told him it was the First Amendment to express my opinion and he could go to—"

"Oh, Jeremy." Just when she thought things were improving, they took a serious detour toward Getting Worse.

Riley clapped Stace on the back. "Don't worry, Stace. I got expelled three times. And I turned out okay."

Jeremy's face perked up. "Really? What'd you do?"

"Do not talk to him," Stace said to Riley. "Not one word." She crossed to her nephew and stood between the two of them like a human shield for bad advice. But she was too late. Jeremy scooted around her and strode up to Riley, beaming up at the playboy like he was seeing a personal hero.

Stace had prayed for another male influence to come

into Jeremy's life. Someone who could speak to him on his level, maybe even take him to the amusement park or play football or any of the things that Frank didn't have the time or the energy to do.

Riley McKenna was the last person she would have picked for the job. And now, watching Riley and Jeremy talk—and her nephew smile for the first time in for-ever—Stace realized she was stuck with her worst nightmare. At work, and now, at home.

Somehow, Stace had to get rid of Riley. As she hus-tled her nephew out of the diner, she vowed to make sure the bachelor was gone by the end of the day tomorrow.

CHAPTER FOUR

RILEY had no business being here. He should have gone to his grandmother's house, to try to talk Gran out of her crazy idea. Or gone to hang out with his friends, who were undoubtedly several beers deep into their evening out already.

Instead Riley found himself flipping through a phone directory, then taking the train several stops down the Red Line until he arrived on the outskirts of Dorchester. Then a long, brisk walk to reach a neighborhood dotted with security bars over the store windows and battered No Trespassing signs nailed to the front of abandoned houses. He took a right, then a left, and another right before finally arriving before an aging one-story Cape with a sagging front porch and peeling white paint.

Riley checked the address he'd jotted down. Checked it again.

This was where Stace lived, according to the phone book. He thought of the guest house he lived in on Gran's property. It wasn't anything grand, but the Newton house and accompanying land were a far cry from the dilapidated building before him.

He wondered again how someone could work the job she did, for the pittance she received, and still be happy.

All those years of sports cars and women and parties, Riley had told himself he was happy.

But now he wasn't so sure that was true. Even though she faced the usual stresses involved in working a hard job, at the end of the day, when she was humming along to the radio, or giving him or Frank a good razzing, he saw something in Stace. A contentment, with her life, her job, herself. So he'd come here tonight, in part, to find a little of that for himself.

And maybe brainstorm a little. He'd been thinking about the diner's struggles over the last few days and had jotted down a few ideas, fiddled with some concepts. Maybe he could put something he'd learned at McKenna Media to work.

The front door flew open and Jeremy burst onto the porch. "Just stay out of my life!" he shouted, then gave the door a slam that threatened to bring down the entire structure. Jeremy stomped down the stairs, then halted when he saw Riley. "What are you, a stalker?"

"Nah." Riley gave the boy a grin. "I was in the neighborhood."

Jeremy looked him up and down, taking in the dress shirt, the pleated pants, the shiny dress shoes. "Sure you were."

"So, did you have a fight with your mom?" he asked Jeremy.

"She's not my mom. She's just my aunt." Jeremy wrinkled his nose in distaste. "All she does is ruin my life."

"By insisting you go to school?"

"Yeah. Like, who needs school? They don't teach me anything I'm going to use." Jeremy dropped onto the porch and rested his elbows on his knees. "School's stupid anyway. All I want to do is draw. Not learn algebra."

"Hey, I used to say the same thing." Riley waved to the space next to Jeremy and when the boy nodded, he sat down beside him. "I skipped school every chance I got, and got to know the principal on a first-name basis."

Jeremy let out a little laugh. "Yeah, me, too."

"Remind me to tell you about the time I smuggled in a chicken and let it loose. On the third floor. In the middle of schoolwide testing."

Jeremy's eyes widened. "You did? Man, what happened?"

"I got expelled. That was expulsion number three, by the way." Riley picked up a pile of grass that had landed on the stairs after a recent mowing and spun it between his fingers. "That was my wake-up call. Well, that and my grandmother's lecture."

"Your grandma? Man, that must have been harsh. What'd your mom and dad say?"

Riley flung the piece of grass at the sidewalk. It fluttered to the chipped concrete, a spiral of green, before slipping between the wide gray crack and disappearing. "My folks died when I was a kid. So me and my brothers went to live with my grandparents. And I gotta tell you, no one can lecture like my grandmother."

"You *have* met Aunt Stace, haven't you?" Jeremy said.

Riley chuckled. "Well, she's only lectured me a little. And I bet she only lectures you because she wants the best for you."

"Yeah, right." The boy got to his feet and leaned against the porch post. His gaze scanned the run-down neighborhood, the houses crying for some TLC. "If this is the best, I'd hate to see the worst."

"It'll work out," Riley said.

Jeremy snorted. "Oh yeah? How do you know that

for sure? You barely know me, man. My father's dead, my mother's a drug addict and all my aunt seems to worry about is whether I'm passing English. You have no idea how my life will work out."

Before Riley could respond, Jeremy thundered down the stairs and took off, a sullen figure in a dark sweatshirt disappearing into the gathering twilight.

The door squeaked behind him. Stace stepped out onto the porch and shot Riley a glare. "What did you say?"

"That you're the meanest woman in Boston."

"You did not."

"Nope, I did not." He got to his feet and tossed her a grin. "I was giving him advice."

She raised a skeptical brow.

"Ask him yourself."

She let out a long breath and her gaze went to the street that had swallowed Jeremy in the growing dark. "If he comes back."

"He will." Riley barely knew this boy, or this woman, so he wasn't entirely positive. Still, he'd had the feeling that underneath all the teenage anger, Jeremy loved his aunt and needed her. Riley stepped farther onto the porch, closer to Stace, and for the first time, noticed the dusting of shadows under her eyes, the lines of worry on her face. "Hey, you want to get something to eat? I had some ideas I wanted to talk over with you."

"Ideas? About what?"

"The diner. I thought if we sat down over some steaks…" Then he thought of the paltry pile of tips in his pocket, and realized he barely had enough to feed himself, never mind another human. "I forgot. I'm broke."

She snorted. "You? Right."

"Seriously."

She eyed him, her gaze penetrating his. "You really are serious."

He held up a palm. "As a heart attack."

"You're really broke?"

"Well, unless you count the coupled hundred dollars I've made so far this week, all of which has to go to rent, yeah."

He thought of his friends. He could hang with them, talk them into covering his dinner, but just the thought of it made him feel bored. Depressed even. He could go home to the guest house, but the space seemed so... empty right now. Hell, it always seemed empty, which was probably why he was more often at his grandmother's than at his own place.

"Anyway," he said, "I was in the neighborhood and thought maybe we could talk about some ideas I had for the diner. But you're busy, so I'll just see you at work." Then his stomach rumbled, like the punctuation to his sentence.

Stace chewed on her lower lip. She glanced down the street, then back at her house, before finally swinging her gaze back to Riley. "I've got a lasagna in the oven. You're welcome to stay."

"Lasagna?" His stomach growled in anticipation. "You're speaking my language, honey."

"Don't call me 'honey' and I might just let you have seconds." She laughed, then pulled open the front door. "I'm probably going to regret this."

He paused in the doorway to lean down close to her ear. "Probably," he whispered.

With the next breath Riley inhaled the sweet and spicy notes of her perfume, and wondered if he was the one making the mistake. But then the scent of lasagna caught him, like a breeze opening the door to the home he'd never really had, and he entered.

The man was a distraction.

Stace had always prided herself on being practical and smart. On making sensible decisions based on careful planning. *Impetuous* would be the last adjective anyone would use to describe Stace Kettering. Then why had she gone and invited a man to dinner on the spur of the moment? A man who was essentially a stranger? A man who was exactly the kind of man she knew better than to get close to?

Hadn't she learned her lesson with Jim? All those wasted years, thinking she was going to marry her childhood sweetheart, only to find out he was about as faithful as a bee in a rose garden. She'd steered clear of the same kind of self-centered man ever since.

Until now. Because every time she talked to Riley, she wondered if maybe there was more to him than the charming facade. Frank was a good judge of character, and if he said there were, there probably was. Riley had, after all, stuck it out so far this week, and that alone told her there might be more to him than just a handsome face. And darn if that handsome face didn't distract her all the time. Had her thinking about him when they weren't together and wondering what he was doing. So yes, a part of the invitation had been curiosity. That was all.

"Do you want something to drink?" She crossed to the fridge and pulled on the handle. "Lemonade? Iced tea?"

"Surprise me."

Surprise him? Like he'd surprised her by showing up here? She still wondered how and why he'd come, but instead of asking, she pulled out the pitcher of lemonade and poured two glasses. She handed one to Riley. "If it's too tart, let me know. Jeremy says I never add enough sugar."

"Tart? Like you?" He grinned.

"I'm sweet." Why was she arguing the point with him? Every time he was around, he brought out this other side of her. A lighter side. She didn't know if that was good or bad.

He laughed. "Of course you are."

"Hey, be nice. Or I won't feed you."

"Yes, ma'am." Riley grinned, then held up the glass. Lemon slices tangoed with ice cubes, and the pale yellow liquid shimmered in the overhead light. "Homemade?"

She nodded.

He took a long sip. "This is...perfect."

"Thanks. Frank says I'm only good at two things. Making drinks and making lasagna." Why was she telling him so much? Was it that she was nervous, having a man in her house, for the first time in...

Well, forever?

Or was some masochistic part of her interested in, and tempted by, Riley McKenna? She kept being lured into joking with him, befriending him...and telling herself she shouldn't do either.

He glanced around her kitchen, and for a second, she wanted to apologize for the outdated appliances, the worn countertops, the scuffed floor. The house had seen better days, many, many years ago, and as much as Stace knew she should move on—

She hadn't.

It was the house she'd lived in all her life, and a part of her couldn't give it up, despite its flaws. "The lasagna should, ah, be done in a couple minutes. Let me just, ah, set a place for you." She crossed to the cabinets again, withdrawing a plate, then silverware. She spun back to the table, but Riley blocked her path.

"You've waited on enough people today." He gently took them from her hands, and nodded toward the table. "You sit. I'll get this."

She let out a nervous chuckle. "I don't know if I should. I've seen you wait tables, remember?"

"Hey, that plate of spaghetti was slippery. And the woman I spilled it on was pretty understanding, considering."

'That's because you flirted with her."

"I did not."

Stace scoffed. "Riley McKenna, you are the biggest flirt I have ever met."

He cocked a smile at her, the same smile that had charmed the customer and made her forget all about the pasta on her skirt. "Hey, she left me a tip in the end."

"And her phone number?"

He grinned. "A gentleman never kisses and tells."

"Gentleman. Right." She reminded herself again not to fall for him. He didn't want her—she was merely a challenge he had yet to win. She was as far from his type as the earth was from Mars. Did he see her as a pity case? Or did he want to butter her up so she wouldn't complain when he slacked off at work tomorrow? Or worse, quit, and left both Frank and her in the lurch?

Because if there was one thing she suspected about Riley, it was that he didn't seem much for sticking. To anything. Or anyone.

He laid out the place settings. The oven timer began to beep, and before Stace could pop out of her chair, Riley had opened the door. He stood there for a second, looking at the hot pan. Stace laughed. "On the counter to your right. Unless you want to burn your hands."

He grabbed the oven mitts, then put them on his hands. "Did you pick pink just for me?"

"Of course." She bit back a smile at the incongruous sight of the tall, dark-haired man with the oversize bright pink mitts on his hands. For the second time, he'd insisted on doing all the work and letting her relax. She had to admit, it was nice, and had her intrigued. Who was Riley McKenna?

He pulled out the lasagna, laid it on the hot plate on the table, then shut the oven again and returned to the table with a spatula and the bowl of salad from the counter.

"Your dinner is served, miss."

"I could get used to this." Stace leaned back in her chair, while Riley dished salad into her bowl. "You're really getting the hang of waiting tables."

"It's a temporary situation. I have no intention of making that a permanent job," he said as he took his seat.

"Moving on to bigger and better things soon?"

Riley toyed with his silverware. "I can't exactly make a career out of working at a diner. I need to find something else."

"Something other than busing tables."

"I didn't mean there's anything wrong with your job—"

"It's okay. I get it. You're saying I should keep the Help Wanted sign in the window. And not depend on you."

"I'm not quitting tomorrow, you know."

"No, but you are quitting someday." All the more reason not to get attached to him. He was just like all the rest, and she'd do well to remember that. She'd feed him, then get back to her real goal—keeping the Morning Glory going and her nephew on track.

Stace cast a worried look down the hall. The front door had yet to open. Chances were good that Jeremy would stay out until it was time for bed. More and more, her nephew did his level best to ignore her. "He's not back yet."

Riley's hand met hers on the table, not touching, just…there. She didn't know how to read that. Every time she thought she had Riley figured out, he did something that didn't fit her definition of selfish playboy.

"Don't worry," he said. "If Jeremy is anything like I was at that age, he'll be here when his stomach is rumbling."

"I hope so." Riley didn't know Jeremy, though, or Stace, really. He couldn't predict the comings and goings of an angry teenager who felt betrayed by his parents and the world.

And neither, it seemed, could Stace. She sighed again, then reached for the dressing and poured some onto her salad, before passing the bottle to Riley. She cut a slice of lasagna, gave herself one, then repeated the action for Riley. The repetitive, ordinary actions of serving dinner kept the worry about Jeremy at bay.

"How did you end up raising Jeremy?" Riley asked. Then he cast an apologetic smile at her. "Sorry. I'm just curious. My grandparents raised me and my brothers after my parents died, and I always wonder when I find other kids in similar situations."

The personal tidbit surprised her. Since she'd met him, he hadn't exactly been Mr. Open about his personal life. Once again, she wondered if her perceptions of Riley—largely formed by overhearing his phone con-

versations or what she'd seen in the gossip columns—
might be a bit skewed. Or if this was merely a ploy to
get close to her—and into her bed. She thought of telling him it was none of his business, but didn't. She'd
been carrying this burden herself for so long. Maybe if
she just talked it out, she could relieve some of the tension of the last few weeks. "Jeremy moved in with me
a month ago after my sister left."

"Left?"

Stace's gaze went to the window, as if that would
suddenly show her a peek of where Lisa was and what
she was doing right now. "She couldn't handle it anymore," Stace said quietly. "So she left."

"Jeremy mentioned she was on drugs," Riley said,
his voice soft, concerned. And the sound opened a window in Stace's heart.

Stace nodded. Tears blurred her vision. "I've tried to
help her a hundred times, but it's never worked. She's
younger than me, and I think losing our mom when we
were young impacted her a lot more than me. Then after
my dad died, she fell in with the wrong crowd—and I
could never get her out of that. Then last month she got
into a car accident with Jeremy in the car, and I guess
that was the last straw for her. She hitched a ride out of
town and I haven't heard from her since."

In an odd way, it was liberating to talk about her sister, and her worries with Jeremy. She hated to burden
Frank any more than she already had, and having Riley
here to listen was…nice.

Riley handed her the basket of garlic bread. "Maybe
she'll come back."

"Maybe." It seemed all Stace did was wait for people to come back. She should have learned her lesson

by now. Staying in the same house, wishing the same wishes, didn't make them come true.

She was just starting to unwrap the towel keeping the bowl of garlic bread warm when she heard the front door open. Jeremy's heavy footfalls sounded in the hall. "I'm hungry. Did you make dinner, Aunt Stace?" he called.

Maybe they did, Stace thought. Maybe they did. She raised her gaze to Riley's and gave him a smile. "You were right."

He grinned, a grin as friendly and open as his words earlier. "It happens."

"I'm glad."

"Me, too." His blue eyes met hers. They seemed warm, comforting. Understanding. "Very glad."

CHAPTER FIVE

THREE voice mails, four texts, and two emails. All from Riley's friends, wondering where the hell he was. The general consensus—he must be dead, because he wasn't sitting in a bar, or out with the woman of the day.

Riley closed the phone and tucked it away. The siren call of his friends didn't speak to him this time. The invitations didn't lure him into the night. Instead, he stayed at Stace Kettering's kitchen table and listened to her tell Jeremy an anecdote about a trio of female customers who'd come into the Morning Glory solely to eat one of every dessert on the menu, for breakfast. "That's how they celebrate their birthdays—dessert for breakfast, lunch, and dinner for the whole day, with lots of shopping in between," Stace said. "They were loud and funny, and a blast to wait on. They left me a Macy's gift card for a tip." Stace pulled it out of her back pocket. "I see some shopping in my future."

He watched the happy animation on Stace's face, while he ate the lasagna she'd baked, and wondered why he stayed here, in her house, and kept going back to the diner when he could have been scouring the classifieds for a better paying job.

His gaze went to the artwork hanging on the walls. Pictures of warriors, of landscapes, of military scenarios, all drawn by Jeremy, who had signed each one with a large, looping *J*. The boy had a good eye, a clear understanding of perspective, and an imaginative mind. He reminded Riley of himself at that age. A dreamer, always doodling and creating.

He glanced over at Stace, who was laughing and moving her hands as she talked, and wondered how she made it on her wages. No wonder she lived in this tiny house that shivered in the wind. Given how slow the diner had been, if she made even twice what he had today, heck, five times, she could hardly afford to eat, never mind pay rent in Boston.

And neither could he.

Granted, he could go to his grandmother, offer her a puppy dog face, and lots of apologies, and be back in Gran's good graces before the day was out. As paltry as those dollars in his pocket were, they were his. He'd earned them. He'd worked hard and he'd been rewarded for his labor.

Such a simple thing, really, to do some work and get paid for it. He'd gotten too used to just showing his face and collecting a paycheck he hadn't earned. Oh, sure, he tossed out an idea or two here and there, sat through a few meetings, and was called in to finesse a client from time to time, but he hadn't really worked at McKenna Media. Hell, the company got more productivity from the potted ficus in the lobby.

It was a new feeling, one that had his mind spinning in new directions. What if he had a job that challenged him? Made him feel productive, rewarded? He'd often heard his brothers talking about serving a purpose, and he'd always thought they were crazy.

Truth be told, Riley hadn't had anything close to a purpose in...well, in a long, long time. Maybe it was time to get that feeling back. The question was how. Maybe if he applied a little of what he'd picked up at McKenna Media at the Morning Glory, it'd be a start.

He glanced at Stace and realized why she loved her job. To her, it was a purpose. What purpose, he didn't know, but he could see the commitment and satisfaction in her every move at the Morning Glory. The problem with purposes, though, was that they made you get involved. Care. Connect.

And Riley made it a personal rule not to do any of the above. Not anymore.

Except, in this tiny little house in Dorchester, it was impossible not to connect. They were nearly elbow-to-elbow at the table, and it felt more like a family than at any dinner Riley had ever attended. The feeling both chafed and welcomed him.

"I'm not going back there," Jeremy said, interrupting Riley's thoughts. Clearly, the subject had changed at some point. The teenager got to his feet so fast, his chair let out a sharp screech and a thick black mark on the floor. "So stop asking me about stupid school. I'm leaving." He stomped out of the kitchen. A few seconds later, the door slammed and Jeremy was gone.

Stace sighed. She opened her mouth to say something, shut it again, then crossed to the sink with her dishes. Riley got up to join her. Outside the window, the skies had turned dark and ugly and a rumble of thunder shook the sky. "You okay?"

She nodded. "I was doing good until I mentioned school. He just doesn't understand the importance of an education."

"Want me to talk to him? I might be able to help. Sometimes the odd man out has a good idea."

She chuckled while she retrieved a plastic container from the cabinet. "Words of wisdom from you?"

"Nah, my grandfather. He was always spouting off some saying or another. It was like living with Confucius. And my father..." Riley shrugged. He didn't want to go there. "Anyway, just call it a bit of McKenna wisdom."

Stace laughed. Then she sighed. "Okay, if you think you can pull some rabbit out of a hat I haven't tried yet, you're welcome to try."

He considered making her a promise, then didn't. He hadn't come here to get more involved with the sassy waitress and her angry nephew. He was here to share ideas about boosting the diner's revenues. Trouble was, he kept forgetting to get around to the topic.

Together they cleaned up dinner, stowing leftovers in the fridge, then loading dishes into the soapy sink water. Riley thought how odd it was that this ramshackle place could feel so much more like home than the guest house he'd lived in since he was nineteen. Low-rent or not, it had a lived-in feel and a warmth about it that he liked.

And that was dangerous. He put his back to the counter. *Get back on track, stop letting this little house tempt you down the wrong path.* "Now that dinner's over, maybe we could sit down and brainstorm some ways to increase business at the diner. I've noticed it's been a little slow and—"

"Why are you doing this?" She crossed her arms over her chest. The easy mood between them arced with tension. "You're not staying. You told me yourself. So don't worry one bit about the Morning Glory. Frank and I have kept it running for a long time before you and we will after you leave, too."

He pushed off from the sink and studied her. "Why is it so hard for you to accept help?"

A second, louder rumble of thunder interrupted them, and then a rainstorm burst from the clouds, sending a fast rush of rain pounding onto the house, sounding like an invading army of ants marching across the shingles. The water slashed against the windows in wet, fast-moving highways. "Oh, damn!" Stace said.

She spun away, jerking open cabinet doors and tugging out two huge pots, and a trio of large plastic bowls. She thrust one of the bowls into Riley's hands. "To the right of the stairs with this one. And this one—" she shoved another bowl at him "—goes in the middle of the living room floor."

"What? Why?" But just as he said the words, he saw the reason—water had started dripping through the ceiling in the kitchen. Stace shoved a pan under the drip to catch the water, which hit the stainless steel bottom with a steady *ping-ping-ping*.

A couple of minutes later, they had the bowls and pots in place. The rain created a symphony inside the house, high-pitched pings and low bass plops. Riley glanced up at the massive polka dots of water stains on the ceiling. "You need a new roof," he said.

"And a new furnace. And new windows. And new appliances." She spread her hands and sighed. "There's not an inch of this house that doesn't need something or other. But the budget only goes so far, and right now, it's been eaten up by the leaky faucet I had to have repaired last week."

The rain continued outside, bolstered by a strong wind that seemed determined to blow the house down. The kitchen window shuddered, and the back door creaked. The symphony became louder, deeper, as the containers filled and the rain continued unabated.

"You should sell this place. It's damp and drafty and—"

"Mine. I happen to love it here. And it's not that bad. When the rain stops—"

A crash sounded down the hall, followed by two thuds and what sounded like a minor tidal wave. Riley and Stace ran to the sound, skidding to a stop outside of Stace's bedroom. Like the rest of the house, her bedroom was decorated in light, cheery colors—a sea blue, with white trim and a butter-yellow comforter on the bed. Or what used to be a butter-yellow comforter on the bed.

"I didn't know you were putting in a skylight."

She smacked his arm. "That is not even remotely funny. What am I going to do?"

He took in the scene before him—a gaping hole in the ceiling, open straight to the stormy sky. Broken shingles, crumpled Sheetrock, rotted framing, piled in a heap on the bed, in the middle of a growing pond. "You're going to have to go to a hotel or something tonight. You can't stay here now. I'll put something over the roof for tonight, and call a contractor in the morning."

Stace snorted. "You. Put something on the roof?"

"I'm handier than you think."

"No, I think *I'm* handier than *you* are."

"Are you saying I don't look the part of a handyman?"

Her gaze roamed over him. "Not at all."

"And why is that?"

"You're too…" She stopped talking. Her face colored. "Well, good-looking."

His grin widened. Did Stace Kettering like him? Or was he reading too much into a simple comment? "You think I'm good-looking?"

"I think *you* think you are." The fists went back on her hips, and her chin rose in defiance. "And well...you don't strike me as the construction type." She pulled one of his hands toward herself and turned it over. "Look. No calluses."

Her touch surprised him. Warm, soft, delicate, it sent a rush through his veins, and for a moment he forgot about the rain pouring into her bedroom. Hell, forgot his own name. He gently flipped over her palm, and ran his fingers down the tender skin. He wanted to do more, much more. Like kiss her. Hold her. Explore every inch of that peach-soft skin. "And this tells me you work too hard," he said quietly.

She glanced down at her hands, then back up at him, her green eyes wide. "I...I have to. I...have bills to pay."

"And that roof to fix." He ran his thumbs over her palm, his fingers over the back of her hand. The light floral notes of her perfume drifted up to tease his senses. Why had he never noticed how soft her hands were before? Or how her eyes were as bright and green as new spring grass?

"Yeah, the...the roof." She pulled away from him and turned back to survey the damage. The moment was gone. Disappointment washed over Riley. "Damn. What am I going to do?"

"Point me in the direction of the garage." He put up a hand to cut off her protest before she could voice it. "I'll take care of putting a tarp on the roof. You clean up the mess here. Anything you can't lift or do, I'll help you with. If we work together, we can get it done faster," he added, using her words from before.

She gave him another dubious glance, then finally nodded. "Garage entrance is in the hall outside the kitchen."

Riley headed out to the one-car garage, and flicked on the light switch. A small puddle in the corner pointed to another leaky spot, but overall, he found the space neat and clean. A compact older model two-door car sat to one side of the garage while a peg board and pair of shelves held assorted gardening and home repair tools on the opposite side. It took Riley a few minutes but he found a tarp, a hammer, some nails, and a ladder. He bundled several long, thin scraps of wood up with the tarp, then tied the whole thing in a bundle with a rope. Then he lifted the garage door and headed out into the rain.

He nestled the ladder against the side of the house, tucked the tarp under one arm, put the hammer and nails into his pockets, and reached out to climb the ladder with his free hand. He got four rungs up before he heard a voice behind him.

"What are you, Santa Claus now?"

Riley turned. Jeremy stood to the side of the ladder, shoulders hunched, his head tucked under a damp sweatshirt hood. Rain pelted his thin frame, darkened his gray sweatshirt.

"I'm fixing your aunt's roof," Riley said. "Temporarily."

"Why?"

"Because it's raining in her bedroom right now."

Jeremy scoffed. "That's because this house is a piece of junk."

"Yeah, well, instead of complaining about it, you could help me." Riley hadn't dressed for the weather, and the rain had already plastered his button-down shirt to his chest. The sooner he was out of the wet and into the house, the better.

"I'm not climbing up there. I could get hurt."

"Yeah, you could. Or you could help me and maybe learn a thing or two."

Jeremy stood there a moment, wavering. Then he reached for the ladder, and hauled himself up behind Riley. "If someone doesn't help you, you're going to break your neck, and then my Aunt Stace will be all upset."

"I'm not so sure about that," Riley said. "Okay, now be sure to hold on tight, and brace yourself on the roof. Okay?"

Jeremy scowled. "I'm not an idiot."

But Riley noticed the boy took his time climbing to the top, and then a moment to steady his feet on the slippery roof. Thankfully, Stace lived in a one-story house, so the drop wasn't as bad as it could have been. Riley tossed the tarp onto the roof, then gestured to Jeremy. "Go around to the other side. But be careful. This roof is like Swiss cheese."

Jeremy picked his way across the shingles, holding onto one corner of the tarp while using his free hand to help balance himself. He and Riley stood on either side of the hole in the roof, while the rain and wind buffeted them.

Stace looked up at them from down below in the bedroom. Through the hole in the ceiling Riley could see she'd already moved most of the mess off the bed, along with all the ruined bedding, and had placed a large cooler in the center of the bed to catch the falling rain. He bit back a laugh at her efficiency.

"Hey!" she shouted. "What is Jeremy doing up there?"

"Helping me. He'll be fine. And we'll get it done in half the time."

"But—"

"It'll be okay, Stace," Riley said. "Trust me. Now will you get out of that room before the rest of the roof caves in?"

"I can't. I have to rescue the teacups." She held up two delicate white China mugs, their fragile faces decorated with bright flowers and gold trim. "I keep meaning to put them on a shelf, and they're just sitting on my dresser. They're going to get crushed by the roof, if another piece falls in."

"Leave them. We'll get them later," Riley said. Beneath his feet, the roof bounced up and down like a sponge. "You gotta get out of that room."

"I will," Stace promised. "Just give me a minute. I can't leave them here."

"Stace—"

Jeremy laid a hand on him. "Let her get them. She's got this thing about those mugs. Her mom gave them to her or something."

So Stace Kettering was a bit sentimental. Clearly, she was about the diner, and now, the teacups. Riley smiled to himself about that, then refocused on saving the roof. Riley and Jeremy unfurled the rest of the tarp, then laid it against the roof. The wind argued and nipped at the edges, trying to tear the tarp out of their hands, but Jeremy held tight while Riley hurried to nail down the strapping. He came around to Jeremy's side and handed the young boy the hammer. "Here." Riley had to shout to be heard over the wind. "You can do this side."

"Me? I don't know how to do that."

"All the more reason why you should." Riley bent down and gestured to Jeremy to do the same. The rain protested even more. "Lay the wood over the tarp, a few inches in so it has something to hold onto. Place the nail between your fingers, then hammer. As soon as the nail has a bite, move your fingers out and send it home."

Jeremy hesitated. Riley nudged the hammer into his palm. "You can do it. I'll be right here."

"I've never done anything like this." Jeremy turned toward Riley. The falling rain ran down his face, soaked his hair. "What if I mess it up?"

The words rocketed Riley back nearly eighteen years. *But, Dad, what if I mess it up?*

You won't, his father had said. He'd laid a tender hand on his son's shoulder. *I'm right here to help you. Riley, if you're always afraid of messing up, you'll never try anything. So...try.*

"It's a tarp and some nails. You can't mess it up. Believe me." Riley handed Jeremy a nail, then laid a piece of wood on top of the blue plastic.

Jeremy hesitated. "I don't know."

"If you're always afraid of messing up, Jeremy, you'll never try anything new." The words his father had said to him so many years ago felt odd coming out of Riley's mouth. Odd, but right. "It'll be okay. I'm right here. Go ahead."

Jeremy did as Riley instructed. His first strike with the hammer was tentative, barely brushing the flat head. Then he hit it harder, and when the nail sank in, he flinched his fingers out of the way and hammered again. Once, twice, three times, until the nail head lay flush against the wood. He looked up at Riley, and a grin broke across his face. "I did it."

"Yep. Now do it a whole lot more. So we can get the heck out of the rain."

The two of them worked together for a few minutes

more, securing the tarp against the roof. When they were done, Riley helped Jeremy down the ladder first, then followed behind him. Stace was waiting at the bottom, bundled up in a bright red Red Sox rain poncho that dwarfed her small frame. She held the bottom of the ladder, worry etched in her features. "Jeremy, you shouldn't have gone up there. If you fell—"

"I was fine, Aunt Stace. I nailed down the tarp," Jeremy said. "Riley showed me how."

"You did? That's awesome, Jeremy." A smile broke across Stace's face. She put a hand on her nephew's arm. "Thank you. I appreciate you doing that."

The boy shrugged. "It was no big deal." He was doing his level best to affect the attitude of an surly teenager again, but it was conflicting with his clear satisfaction and self-pride for a job well done.

"It was a *huge* deal," Stace said, then mouthed a thank-you to Riley, too. "Come on, let's get you guys inside and dried off."

The three of them headed into the house, back to the symphony of raindrops. The temperature in the little house had begun to drop. The tarp would keep the rain out, but it was a temporary fix, and the wind still nipped beneath the plastic cover like an unwelcome visitor.

Jeremy headed to the bathroom to take a hot shower, leaving Riley and Stace alone in the kitchen. She pressed a hand to his shirt. His heart tripped at her warm, comforting...no, perfect touch. Delicate, yet also strong fingers, awakening parts of him that shouldn't be awake. Not when he was trying to keep this platonic. He was leaving, as he'd said.

"Thank you," she said. "You didn't have to do that."

"No, I didn't, but I did. To help you out."

The room closed in on them, tighter, smaller than

five minutes before. "You're, uh, soaked clear through," she said.

He covered her palm with his own. "It's raining outside."

"There's a storm out there," she said. Her green eyes met his, and her voice dropped into a softer, deeper range. "And in here."

Tension unfurled between them like a roll of twine. He watched her lips move, watched her eyes widen, watched her breath slip in and out of her mouth. He no longer felt the wet, cold fabric plastered against his skin. Instead a growing heat burned inside him. He lowered his head, until his lips were inches from hers. Damn. He wanted her. More now than before, when he'd barely known her. Now he'd tasted her cooking, heard her laugh, seen her smile, and that only quadrupled his desire. "Stace—"

"Here." She thrust a towel against his chest. "You... you should dry off before you get sick."

Riley backed away, took the towel—and the hint—from Stace, and rubbed the soft floral-scented terry cloth over his face, so she wouldn't see the disappointment in his features. For a man who didn't want to get involved, he kept doing that very thing. "Thanks."

"And...I'm sorry for not trusting you about the roof," she said.

He grinned. "Hey, what can I say? I have the hands of a man who does nothing all day."

"I shouldn't have said that. You did a great job with the roof, and my nephew. I appreciate it." She grabbed two cups of coffee from the counter and handed one to Riley. "Jeremy really needs a male influence. Frank is great, but it's nice for him to be around someone closer to his age. Someone who can teach him things." She gave him a self-deprecating grin. "I'm not exactly dad material."

Dad material? Riley McKenna didn't fit those words. Maybe he had made a small impact on Jeremy today, but Riley was sure it would probably be erased as soon as the subject of school or curfew came up.

If anything screamed "woman looking for a commitment," the words *dad material* were it. Riley knew he should stay away, walk out the door right now, and leave Stace and Jeremy to deal with their own lives. After all, he wasn't a man who got involved. Ever. He liked his life the way it was—unencumbered and easy. Except that way of life seemed so...empty lately.

What the hell was wrong with him?

He glanced around the run-down house again, at the half-filled pots of rainwater. And the urge to help just a little bit more roared to life. She wouldn't let him help with the diner but she had here. Jeremy and Stace were in trouble, and a helping hand didn't constitute involvement. It was just being...nice. "You can't stay here. It's freezing and wet, and who knows what will happen with the rest of the roof tonight? Come on back to my house, and then at least you and Jeremy will be warm and dry," he said. "Come on, I'll take you there."

"Please. I'm not..." She put up her hands, then cast a glance down the hall, and lowered her voice. "Interested in a...relationship."

Riley leaned in close. "Neither am I. This is about helping you. Not about sex." Then he took in a breath and caught the sweet floral fragrance wafting off her skin. And a part of him mounted a very vocal campaign for the idea of sex and Stace Kettering.

Stace worried her bottom lip again. "We won't stay more than a night."

"The roof won't be fixed that fast. And they're predicting rain for the next few days."

"I'll find somewhere else to stay. With Frank, or in a motel, or something. I don't want..."

"Want what?"

Her face colored. "We barely know each other."

"What better way to change that situation?" He tossed her a grin, and tried not to wonder why a man who was committed to staying uninvolved, kept getting involved with this woman. "I promise, I don't walk around nude or leave my dirty laundry on the kitchen floor. Most of the time anyway."

A smirk started on one corner of her mouth. "I don't know if it's a good idea."

"Come on, it'll be fun. I promise."

"Fun?" She let out a laugh. "The last time I had fun was probably 1998."

"Then all the more reason to start today. And who better to show you how to have a good time than the man dubbed one of Boston's most eligible bachelors?"

What had she been thinking?

Stace got out of the taxi, and stood in the driveway of the McKenna house. The main home was a stately dark green Victorian, complete with a spiraling turret, long, inviting porch, and crisp white trim. The brick driveway wound around the east side of the house, leading to a smaller version of the main house, a little one-story bungalow with a one-car garage. The guest house.

Where she and Jeremy would be staying with Riley. For at least one night.

How did she go from zero to sixty with this guy in mere days? One minute she was working with him, having dinner with him, and now, she was temporarily *living* with him. Last week, she barely even knew him.

Now she was sharing a bathroom with him.

"We're staying here?" Jeremy looked back at his aunt. "For how long?"

Stace jerked her suitcase out of the back of the car, then hauled Jeremy's bag up and handed it to him. "Don't get too comfortable. It's only temporary. A day or two." Riley opened the door to the guest house and waved at her from the front door. He really was a handsome man. The kind that made her forget all the reasons she had for not getting involved with anyone, and especially not involved with one of the most notorious bachelors in the city. *Especially* not with him. He had heartbreaker written all over him and she kept on overlooking that because he dished up her lasagna or fixed her roof. "We'll be gone before you know it."

"Of course," Jeremy grumbled. "Because why would we want to stay at a place with a pool?"

"He has a pool?"

Jeremy nodded, then pointed to the left of the guest house at a glass enclosure that wrapped around an inground pool. A hot tub flanked one corner, a barbecue and seating area on the other. The entire thing was designed to look like a private lagoon, with big faux boulders and lush greenery. In the middle of Boston, in the middle of fall.

The urge to dive into that sparkling water, to let it wash over her, take away the stress of the last year, rose up inside her. Then she glanced at Riley and an image of an entirely different sort sprung to mind. Him in that water with her, sliding against her body, hands running over her skin—

"We'll be moving out before you know it," Stace

said, more firmly this time. And before she could make a mistake.

The rain had abated—slightly—so she hurried toward the house, her suitcase bumping along the driveway behind her. Jeremy took his time, his hood up over his head, and his gaze roaming the grounds of the house.

A house with grounds. Space. The kind of house she saw on TV all the time, and dreamed about sometimes, but would never own. She wondered again why Riley McKenna had chosen to work at the diner, when clearly, he didn't need to work at all.

"Come on in," Riley said, taking Stace's suitcase from her before she reached the threshold. Jeremy ducked into the bungalow and dumped his bag right inside the door.

"Jeremy, don't leave that there," Stace said.

"He's fine. I'm not a picky housekeeper." Riley stood behind Stace and helped her off with her coat. He turned, hung it in a nearby closet, then gestured to a hall. "It's only a two-bedroom, so I thought you could sleep in the guest room and Jeremy could have the sofa bed."

"With that TV?" Jeremy said, pointing at the bachelor staple—a 50-inch big screen with surround sound.

Riley grinned. "Yep. All yours."

"Until ten," Stace added. "You have to get up in the morning for school."

"I'm expelled, remember? I don't have anywhere to go tomorrow. And nobody who cares where I go anyway," he added in a mumble. Then he flopped onto the couch, picked up the remote, and was flipping through channels in less time than it took Stace to say boo. For the hundredth time, Stace wished her sister was here—

and sober. Jeremy was clearly hurting, and there was so little Stace could do about it.

"Jeremy, you should ask permission before you turn on the television," she said. "This isn't your house."

"He's fine, Stace. Relax." Riley took her arm. "Come on, I'll show you your room. Let you get settled."

She glanced back at her nephew. "I should—"

"Listen to me. You work way too hard."

"Coming from the man who doesn't?"

"Hey, I worked today." He stretched the kinks in his back. "And I'm feeling it now."

She laughed. Apparently he was starting to realize that a day's work in the diner was harder than it looked. "Get used to it. Tomorrow will be worse."

"Why?"

"It's payday. We're always busier on payday than early in the week." She paused as he opened a door and waved her into a small, bright room. A double bed sat square in the center, flanked by two nightstands. The room was painted the color of a robin's egg. A soft beige rug anchored the room, and invited her to sink her toes into the thick plush. A pair of French doors on the far side opened onto a walkway that connected to the sparkling, bright blue waters of the pool. It all looked so inviting, comforting. Wonderful.

"It's not very big," Riley said. "Sorry about that."

"It's perfect." She turned and gave him a smile. "Thank you."

"You're welcome." His smile was warm, and just as inviting and tempting as the room.

The clock on the wall ticked by with the time. In the distance, she could hear the low murmur of the television. The rain pit-patted against the windows. But here, in this space, all she could see, hear, notice, was Riley

McKenna. His ocean-blue eyes seemed to hold her captive, and she stood there, inhaling the spicy notes of his cologne and wondering how those hands she had teased him about would feel against her skin. "Thank you."

"You said that already."

A flash of golden fur ran by outside. "You have a dog?"

"My brother's dog, Heidi. He and his wife are out of town for a couple days and my grandmother's watching her."

"Oh." Stace thumbed toward the closet. "I should probably unpack and get to bed. I mean, to sleep. Busy day tomorrow." God, now she was tripping over words and innuendos. Moving in here *definitely* wasn't a good idea.

He took a step back. Disappointment rushed in to fill the gap. "I'll leave you to it then." He stepped out of the room and shut the door, leaving Stace alone.

She should open her suitcase, hang up her clothes for work tomorrow, lay out her makeup, set up her nightly routine. It was after nine already, and four in the morning came early. She still had to find something to do with Jeremy tomorrow, and a way to get him into school again. Not to mention find the money to fix the roof. While still paying for groceries and electric and tuition.

The responsibilities weighed heavy on Stace's shoulders. She released the suitcase's handle and crossed the room, until she reached the glass doors. For a long while, she just watched the rain fall in shimmering lines.

Then she opened the door, stepped outside, and walked down the path to the pool area. The door opened easily, a wave of moist heat hit her, as comforting as an electric blanket. Stace kicked off her shoes and crossed to the tiled edge. She dipped one toe into the water, and let out a sigh.

"It's as warm as a bath, isn't it?"

Stace jerked away from the edge too fast, and lost her balance. Her arms pinwheeled at her sides and she wobbled on one foot. Before she tumbled into the water, Riley was there, one arm around her waist. He hauled her back onto the tile in a single fast, easy movement, as if she weighed no more than a feather. "Riley! You scared me."

"Sorry." The lights overhead danced across his features, sparkled in his eyes. "You want to take a swim?"

"I can't. I didn't bring a swimsuit."

"My bad. I should have mentioned the pool. I'm hardly ever out here anymore, and sometimes I forget it's here."

"Really? If I had a pool, I'd be in it every day."

"You like to swim?"

"Very much." She sighed. "I was on the swim team and everything. A million years ago."

"Really?" He arched a brow.

"Yeah. It was back in high school. And then…" She wrapped her arms around herself, and turned away. Why had she started talking? She never talked about the past. Never revisited things that couldn't be changed. "Anyway, it was all a long time ago.

"It's been years since I've had regular access to a pool," she said. "I used to go to the Y and do laps in the pool there, but—"

"But what?" he asked, his voice as gentle as the ripples in the water. Urging, coaxing.

"I…I stopped after my father died." She let out a long breath. That was the truth of it. All these years, she told herself she'd quit swimming because she'd been so busy, but really, it was because she had been struggling to stay afloat in her life, and that had consumed all her energy. "I had to step in and work the diner, take care of my sister, my nephew, the house…" She put out her hands.

"And there wasn't any time to take care of you."

"I guess I just put me at the bottom of the list."

"Then today's the day you stop." Riley smiled at her.

Stace shook her head because if she spoke, she was sure tears were going to be falling.

Riley went on, undaunted. "My grandmother likes to bargain hunt so she has a bunch of swimsuits she's bought on sale in the changing room over there." He thumbed toward a door on the right. "I'm sure there's something in your size. Go get one and spend as much time in the pool as you want."

"I really shouldn't. The morning comes awful early." But she couldn't resist taking one look back at the pool, at the slight ripples kissed by pale white light. The water beckoned to her, like a friend.

"Nope, no excuses, Stace." He put a finger under her chin until she was looking at him. "Go ahead and enjoy yourself for once."

"Riley—"

"I'll go in if you will. And best of all the water's heated." Riley bent down, scooped up a handful of water, and drizzled it over her palm. The warm drops slid down her fingers, across her hand. "Now, how can you resist that?"

Two minutes later, Stace found herself standing on the deep end of the pool, dressed in a dark blue one-piece bathing suit that hugged her frame so snugly, there wasn't much left to the imagination. The water sparkled beneath her, and before she could think twice—

Stace leaped up and did a hard, fast cannonball into

the deep end. She plunged to the bottom, the water encasing her in a moment of silence before she popped back up.

"Bravo!"

She whirled around. Riley stood on the side, giving her a thumbs-up. "I'm sorry, I—"

"You had fun. And you did it well. Better than me, I think." He grinned. He was wearing a pair of red-and-black swim trunks, and carrying two towels. Wow. He was just as handsome and tempting unclothed as he was clothed. He had a broad, defined chest, narrowing in a *V* to a flat abdomen and tight waist. She curled her hands at her side because she had the strangest urge to place her palms on the muscled expanse of his chest.

She turned away and dove under the water, skimming down to the bottom then halfway across the pool. The minute the water enveloped her, a sense of peace settled on her shoulders, eased through her body. It was like…

Like coming home.

She forgot about Riley. Forgot about Jeremy. Forgot about the roof. She emerged for one quick breath, then went down again, gliding through the pale blue silent world under the surface. She swam from one end to the other, then rose up for another breath before making the journey a second time.

At the deep end, she came up for air again, and found Riley treading water beside her. "You are a hell of a swimmer," he said.

She shifted to tread water, too, pausing to wipe the hair out of her eyes. She told herself she didn't care how she looked wet—she never had before, and she wasn't going to start now. But a part of her did worry if there was mascara racooning under her eyes, or a tangled birds' nest of hair on top of her head. "Thanks."

His arms slid through the water in easy, practiced moves. His legs moved with a steady rhythm that didn't waste energy. "When I was younger, I spent a lot of hours out here."

"Pool parties with the girls in the neighborhood?"

"Nah. My football coach recommended we swim in the off season to build up our cardio and endurance. My grandfather heard that and put in a pool. I wanted to be the next Joe Namath, so I swam my butt off every winter. My grandfather thought it would build character, and he was right. I was in the water every morning by five, swimming for an hour and a half before school."

"Really? That's commitment."

He leaned in close. "I'm not as awful as you think I am."

"I don't think you're awful. At all." The words were out before she could stop them. What was it about Riley that had her confessing all her deepest thoughts?

"What *do* you think, Stace Kettering?"

"I…I think it's time to get out of the pool. Jeremy—"

"Is asleep. He passed out on the couch earlier. So stay, have some fun."

The water swished over her shoulders, trickled down her back. Droplets spiked on Riley's eyelashes, darkened his hair. "I, ah, should probably get out anyway. Early day tomorrow."

"I know. You keep saying that." He shifted closer to her, so close that she could feel the underwater currents created by his hands and legs. One of his legs brushed against hers, and she told herself to pull back. But she couldn't move. "If I'm not that awful then why do you do your best to avoid me?"

"I'm not avoiding you. I'm just not interested."

"Really?"

She swallowed. Tried not to look at his chest. "Really."

"So if I kissed you right now, you'd feel…nothing?"

Kiss her? A hot rush of anticipation flooded her. "I…I don't think we should do that."

"Why not? We're two consenting adults. Alone. In a pool. At night."

"I know that." Heck, every nerve in her body knew it. To her very core, Stace was hyper-attuned to Riley. To his bare skin, so close she could touch him with a whisper of movement, to his long legs, his hard chest, his broad shoulders. To everything.

"Then what's holding you back?" He shifted again, and now his legs were sliding against hers, and everything inside her melted.

She opened her mouth to speak, and couldn't. Every sensuous stroke of his skin on hers sent her mind skittering. Made her forget how she'd sworn off men like him.

"I want to kiss you, Stace," he said, his voice dark, low, tempting.

"I…" Her mouth opened. Closed again. "Okay." The word escaped her in a breathless rush.

Riley closed the gap between them. He wrapped one arm around her body. Their legs tangled, their torsos met, and every inch of her skin that connected with his seemed to light on fire. His blue eyes connected with hers, and held for one long heated second before he leaned in to kiss her.

At the same time, their two pairs of legs kicked, and tangled. The kiss became a knocking of chins, and the moment of unbalance sent them both bobbing under the water. Stace came up first, sputtering the unexpected wave out of her face and mouth, then Riley did the same. He looked like a wet puppy, and Stace started laughing. "Well, that wasn't exactly the moment of romance I was expecting," she said.

"Me either." He took her hand, and gave a big kick, dragging them both to shallower water. When they were both standing, he released her hand and cupped her jaw with both his hands. "Let's try that again."

This time, the anticipation roared through her like a train. Desire pooled in her gut, and she knew—knew without a shadow of a doubt—that this would be a kiss she would never forget. But most of all, she knew that letting Riley McKenna kiss her would be the biggest mistake of her life.

A mistake she couldn't afford to make.

CHAPTER SIX

FOR a busy diner, the silence could be deafening, Riley thought.

Stace hadn't talked to him since last night in the pool. She'd scrambled out of the water before he could kiss her, then sputtered something about needing to get to bed and hurried into the house. This morning at the diner, she'd done her job, kept her head down, and done her best to avoid him.

He'd gone out after the pool incident, headed off to barhop with Alec and Bill, staying out way too late, before coming home to collapse on his bed. He'd wasted half the money he'd earned on drinks that had done nothing to help him forget a woman with dancing green eyes. A woman who sang like a bird and did cannonballs like the best teenage boy.

When Riley woke up, Stace had already left for the morning. Jeremy was still asleep on the couch, so Riley had tiptoed around his house. On the kitchen counter, he had found a note from Stace to Jeremy, sitting beside a covered plate of pancakes.

Riley hadn't even known he had pancake mix. For a second, he envied the teenage boy who had someone who loved him enough to make him pancakes before the sun even had a chance to rise. Riley stared at those pancakes for a long, long time, and wondered about the woman who had intrigued him more than any he had ever met before. A woman who had already added a feminine touch to his home with the vanilla-scented pancakes, a floral makeup bag in the bathroom, and a bright yellow sweater draped over the back of a chair. A woman he told himself he didn't want, even as his gaze strayed to her again and again and desire pulsed inside him.

She bustled between the tables with the same efficiency as always, but with a decided distance from Riley. He missed her being at his shoulder, checking on his service, making sure he had the right order in place. He'd gotten used to her being nearby. And to her smile, her banter.

The morning rush passed quickly, though Riley found himself lagging behind several times. By his fourth cup of coffee, he was awake enough to handle the customer influx, and his hangover had abated to a tolerable level. By nine, the diner was empty and Riley heard Frank head out the back door for a bit of fresh air.

Across the room, Stace wiped tables in fast, concentric circles. No humming under her breath this time. Riley snatched up the salt and pepper shakers and held them out of her way. "How long are you going to avoid me?"

"I called a roofer this morning. He'll be out to give me an estimate later today. I'm going to move back to the house and just sleep on the couch until the roof is done and I can replace that mattress."

"You know, you shouldn't have been on the swim team."

She stopped cleaning and looked up at him. "What are you talking about?"

"You should have been on the track team because you are a master runner."

She scowled and went back to work. "I'm not running. I'm being realistic. I don't live with you, Riley. I live in that house in Dorchester, with all its flaws and problems. And I'm not going to date you and become another notch on your bedpost."

"Is that what you think last night was about?"

She straightened and propped a fist on her hip. "Are you going to try to tell me it wasn't?"

Disagreeing would mean telling her he had briefly considered something more. Something like the happiness Finn had found with Ellie. The same happiness his grandparents had enjoyed. But if there was one thing Riley had learned early in life, it was that depending on another person to be there when you needed them most was a foolish thing. So he retreated to his default position. "Well, you know me. Not the kind of guy who speaks the *M* word. Or the *L* one or any of the others in that alphabet of commitment."

A flicker of disappointment ran across her features. "Now that I believe."

For some reason, her assessment stung him. Riley had never been a man who wanted to settle down. Or sought a relationship that lasted longer than the expiration date on a block of cheese. He might envy Finn and his grandparents, but just the thought of those kind of ties made him feel choked.

The problem? Those were the kinds of ties that left pancakes on the counter in the morning.

So he decided to take the easy route. And change the subject. "Did you hear back from Jeremy's school?"

Stace plopped into an empty chair and dropped the rag onto the table. "Yes. I talked to them twice this morning. They're not going to budge on the expulsion. He can't just stay home all day, and the other school in our district is…well, the lowest ranked in the state, and not the safest or best learning environment. I really don't want to send him there." She let out a long sigh.

"Have you thought about Wilmont Academy?"

"Wilmont Academy? I can't afford that." She dropped her head into her hands. "I don't know what I'm going to do."

He laid a hand on her shoulder. The touch was meant to be comforting, friendly even, but it seared Riley's palm and rocketed his mind back to the pool. To the kiss that had ended before it started. He should have followed her last night, damn it. Finished what they barely began. But she'd made it clear she wasn't interested, and he had to accept that. Instead, he could at least help take one worry off her shoulders. "Wilmont might be the perfect thing for him. I went there, and it was a great option for me. I was like Jeremy, creative, a little ornery—"

She laughed. "Perfect adjective for you."

"I saw Jeremy's artwork at the house. I think he'll love it there. And hey, maybe there's a scholarship or something he could get."

"That would take a miracle," she said.

"You never know," Riley said, before turning to wipe the last table. "Miracles have been known to happen."

The last of the lunch crowd began to peter out. Stace's mind went to the pool at Riley's house. How nice it would be to slip into the water, and lose herself for an hour or so, in the mindless strokes of a good swim.

Thinking of the pool led directly to thinking of him. Of how close they had come to kissing. How for a little while, she really, really wanted him to kiss her. Riley McKenna, with his lopsided grin and piercing blue eyes, had gotten under her skin.

And that was trouble.

Stace didn't have time or room for a relationship in her life. She had Jeremy to focus on, then the balance in her bank account, and finally, Frank. She'd been working too hard and too long to save enough money to buy out Frank, and finally get him to retire and take some well deserved time for himself, to get sidetracked now. The roof repair, even with the amount covered by insurance, would take a chunk out of her savings, but if she worked hard, she could make that up.

And that meant staying away from trouble. Particularly trouble that came in a six-foot-two, dark-haired, blue-eyed package. She'd been down that road before and knew it led to heartbreak.

The bell over the door chimed, and a stately elderly woman entered the Morning Glory. She was tall, reed-thin, and had gray hair styled in a soft wave across her head. She wore a long plaid skirt, short heeled shoes, and an oatmeal-colored twinset. She looked like she'd just walked out of a church, or a bridge club. Stace crossed to her, lifting a menu out of the hostess station as she did. "Welcome to the Morning Glory, ma'am," Stace said. "Table for one?"

"For two." The older woman smiled and her gaze went past Stace. "Though I think someone is going to insist on making it for three."

Riley slipped in between them and pressed a kiss to the older woman's cheek. "Gran. You didn't have to make the trip down here."

"I'm not bed-ridden, Riley. I can still get around this city."

He chuckled then he gestured to Stace. "This is Stace Kettering, the best waitress in the city of Boston. Stace, meet my grandmother, Mary McKenna. And in the kitchen is Frank, who can cook you a burger with one hand tied behind his back and his eyes closed."

Mary put out her hand, and when she shook with Stace, her grip was firm and strong. "Pleasure to meet you, my dear."

"You too, Mrs. McKenna." Now that they were together, she could see the family resemblance between Mary and Riley. They had similar bone structure, the same blue eyes, and the same smile.

Riley put out his arm and waited for his grandmother to slip her hand into the crook. "Come on, Gran. Let me show you to the best table in the diner."

"And where is that?" Mary asked.

"Why, the one I'm sitting at, of course." He laughed, and she swatted him, but went along and sat at a corner booth. Windows fronted either side of the table, which made it a favorite among customers who liked to people-watch. It was indeed, as Riley had said, the best table in the Morning Glory, and the one Stace often sat at when the diner was empty and she had a chance to eat a meal or take a break. Riley waited until his grandmother was settled, with her clutch purse seated on the bench beside her. "Do you want some coffee?" he asked.

She arched a brow in surprise. "You're taking my order?"

"That's what they pay me to do." He gave the table a tap. "I'll be right back."

"Here you are, ma'am." Stace handed Mary a menu, and started to turn away when Mary put a hand on her arm.

"Please, sit. I'd like to get to know you." Mary gave

her a kind smile, then waved to the opposite seat. "Tell me. How's my grandson working out?"

Stace slid into the cushioned booth, and let out a sigh of contentment. After a long day of being on her feet, the mere act of pausing was like heaven. "He's doing great. He's learning. I think he's realized it's a harder job than it looks."

"He's a good man." Mary smiled. "And yes, I'm biased."

"That's okay. That's how it is with family." For a second, Stace envied Riley this connection with his DNA. She'd lost her grandparents when she was little, and with both her mother and father gone, there was no real Kettering connection for her anymore. Her sister had checked out long ago, and God only knew where she was now. That left just Jeremy and Stace. She missed family dinners and noisy Christmases. Riley still had that, and had two brothers to add to the mix. She wondered if he realized how lucky he was.

"Speaking of family," Mary said, "is your nephew here? I'd like to meet him. Riley says he deserves a McKenna scholarship."

"He did?"

Mary nodded. "He called me and said you were interested in Wilmont, but couldn't afford it. He told me a little about Jeremy, and said he'd be perfect for the scholarship."

Riley had said maybe a scholarship would come along to pay for the tuition. She'd never thought he meant he'd make that happen. "He said that? Really?" She glanced across the diner, where Riley was pouring three coffees. He'd stepped in to help, even when she'd told him not to. And for some reason, that pleased her. But still, she didn't want Mary to feel obligated to help.

"You don't have to do this just because Riley called. I'm sure we can find a way to handle it ourselves."

Mary laughed. "If there's one thing Riley will tell you about me, it's that nobody forces Mary McKenna to do anything. I'm sure Jeremy will love Wilmont Academy."

'He's not much of a student, I'm afraid."

"Neither was Riley, and that's why that school was perfect."

Riley deposited the coffees on the table. "Gushing about me again?"

"Of course not." Mary's voice was stern but her features soft. "You were a handful, and still are."

"You must be talking about Finn." Riley grinned, then thumbed toward the kitchen. "Are you hungry, Gran? Frank can make anything you want."

"A turkey sandwich would be nice," Mary said.

"Coming right up. With twenty-two fries, not twenty-one." The last he directed at Stace, with a grin, then he was gone.

"Twenty-two fries?" Mary asked.

"Inside joke." Stace found herself smiling. When had she and Riley gone from combative coworkers to friends with inside jokes? She thought of their almost-kiss the night before. Friends? Or maybe…something more?

No, nothing more. A moment of insanity.

After all, hadn't he just made it clear he hated responsibility? His whole life, or at least what she'd seen chronicled in the papers, had been about being irresponsible. The last thing she needed was one more person depending on her to be the grown-up. Jim had done that and it wasn't until he was gone that she'd realized how much she'd been the one to hold everything together.

"I'm glad to see Riley so happy," Mary said, drawing Stace's attention back. "Might I assume that has something to do with you living in the guest house?"

"Oh, no, no, that's a temporary thing. There's a hole in my roof and Riley insisted Jeremy and I stay with him until it's fixed." Stace made sure to emphasize her nephew's name, to remind herself and Mary that it wasn't a living together situation at all, merely a favor. "It's temporary."

"You said that already." Mary smiled and Stace wanted to shrink into the chair and disappear.

Why did she stumble every time she talked about Riley? She wasn't interested in him. At all. He'd gone out last night—which of course was his right, because they were coworkers, not husband and wife—and probably ended up with one of those pretty blondes she'd seen pictured beside him in the paper before.

And Stace wasn't jealous. Not one bit.

No, she was just glad it hadn't been her on his arm. That she'd resisted his kiss. Very glad. Uh-huh. Sure.

As if on cue, Jeremy emerged from the kitchen. He often came in the back door after school to hang with Frank and get a snack, before coming out to greet his aunt. Stace waved him over. Thank God. A reason to change the subject away from Riley McKenna. "Jeremy, this is Riley's grandmother, Mrs. McKenna."

"Hi," Jeremy said. Stace gave him an arched brow. "Uh, nice to meet you."

"She runs the McKenna Foundation," Stace reminded him. "And she told me that they give out a scholarship to the Wilmont Academy."

"That's a really cool school," Jeremy said, his interest piqued now. "I was just talking to one of my friends who goes there. He does photography and he sold a picture to the *Globe*. He's, like, famous now."

Mary patted the table. "Come, sit down, young man. Let me get to know you."

Jeremy did as he was asked, and after a few minutes of easy chatting between Jeremy and Mary, Stace took the cue from Mary and left the two to talk alone. She glanced back over her shoulder at her nephew, who was talking fast, his hands moving in animated excitement. Every time the subject turned to art, Jeremy's entire demeanor shifted from angry to eager and creative. Maybe Riley was right, and this new school would be the right thing to turn her nephew's life around.

She met up with Riley on the other side of the counter, where he was waiting for Frank to finish assembling Mary's sandwich. "Your grandmother is really nice."

"Thanks. And I know she means well when she does things like cut me off financially."

The pieces fell into place. Riley saying he was broke. Applying for jobs. Taking the one here. "That's what happened?"

Riley nodded. "Yup, that's why I'm here. She told me to get out there, pay my own way and truly earn my keep."

"But I thought you worked for the family business."

"Used to. And I didn't really do anything much." He gestured to the diner, and a measure of respect filled his features. "*This* is work. I don't know how you do it."

"I just do." She shrugged. "I have bills to pay, and I just suck it up and work hard."

"Well, I admire you."

Heat rushed to her cheeks, and she had to look away. "Thanks." His praise pleased her, more than she wanted to admit. Every minute she spent with Riley revealed another dimension to the man. Was he the fun-loving rich kid who shrugged off the word *responsibility* like a horsehair shirt? Or this Riley, who recognized hard work, loved his family, and helped out people he barely knew?

Riley leaned in close. "I have to tell you that I'm sorry for not being a good customer. If I'd gotten me, I'd have dumped a hot pot of coffee in my lap."

She laughed. "I was tempted. Many times."

"Well, next time, feel free." Then he glanced at the percolating pot. Steam rose from the brewing coffee. "On second thought, ice water might be better."

"I'll remember that."

"I bet you will." He laughed.

She gave Riley a light slug in the arm. "I'm kinda getting used to you being around here. You're becoming part of the Morning Glory Diner." And a part of her liked that, whether she wanted to admit it or not.

His gaze went past her, to the street outside, or to something else, she couldn't tell. "Well, before you know it, I'll be out of your hair, and back to being just a customer." He took the sandwich that Frank had laid on the counter and turned toward his grandmother's table. "So keep that ice water handy."

She watched him go. He lingered only a moment, exchanging a few words with Jeremy, and then his grandmother before he returned to where Stace was standing.

"Looks like Jeremy's got a new school to attend," Riley said.

"Really? Your grandmother approved him for the scholarship?"

He nodded. "It lasts as long as he attends. He does have to keep his grades up, though. Gran added that stipulation after I graduated. Apparently I set a bad example for the other kids." Riley grinned. "But you won't have to pay for anything."

"That's just…too much. I can't—"

"You can." His hand lingered on her back for a moment more.

Tears welled in her eyes, and before she could think twice, she flung her arms around him. "Thank you. You have no idea what this means."

He held her tight and thought of the pancakes, then he smiled into her hair and inhaled the scent of vanilla, lavender and a sweet goodness that he had never known before. "I think I do."

It also meant Riley was in deep. And he had a feeling he was going to be able to tread water for only so long.

CHAPTER SEVEN

ALL it took to trip the switch in Riley was a quartet of needy, demanding customers who complained loudly and often about the service, the food and even the napkins. They left Riley with a quarter for a tip, and an attitude.

He watched them leave, and the old familiar urge to run rose inside him. He'd left a half dozen jobs...no, more...because he hadn't found one he loved. And he sure as heck didn't love this one. What had Stace said earlier?

He was becoming part of the Morning Glory Diner.

When she'd said that, he'd realized she was right—he'd been connecting with the diners, to her, to her nephew. He was *bonding,* for Pete's sake. He'd gone and involved his grandmother, and helped not just Stace, but her nephew, too.

All Riley had wanted was a job. With no attachments.

This was a temporary position, a transition of sorts, not a permanent place for him to settle down. He bristled at the thought of being part of anything. Riley didn't do attached, and he wasn't about to start now. The whole thought of being here in a month, a year, heck, a decade, threatened to suffocate him.

So when Alec called with an invitation to lunch at

the club, the urge to return to the fancy, devil-may-care life he'd had before nagged at Riley. Shrug off these responsibilities and expectations for an hour. And away from Stace Kettering, who drew him in like a magnet every time he said he wanted distance.

Stace passed by him, a loaded tray balanced on one shoulder. "Don't worry about those customers. We all get bad apples from time to time."

"Yeah." Riley glanced at the clock, then the nearly empty diner, and had the apron strings undone and the yoke of his job tossed onto a nearby chair in the next second. "Hey, I'm going to go out to grab a bite to eat," he said to Stace. "Is that okay?"

"Sure. Just be back soon. I was hoping to get out of here early. Remember, I have the roofer coming by to give me an estimate."

"No problem." Relief surged in his chest, like loosening a set of chains.

Stace sent him a smile, and a ribbon of guilt ran through him. He shrugged it off. He had a right to a social life. He wasn't married to Stace, or to this job. And he sure as hell wasn't "responsible" or purposed or committed or any of the other things his grandmother and everyone around him seemed to think he should be. He deserved a lunch out with Alec. Some time where no one wanted coffee or checks or anything from him.

Responsible men settled down. Had families. Built stuff in the garage. He'd done enough of that in the past few days, and it was leading him down a dangerous path of doing more.

He wasn't going to be that kind of man. Ever. And the sooner Stace realized that, the better.

* * *

Stace refused to talk to him. Riley had returned to the diner a little after three, and found her finishing the cleanup alone. She didn't greet him when he walked in the door, and brushed him off when he offered to stack chairs. The afternoon's meal with Alec, in an overpriced club eating an overpriced sandwich accompanied by an overpriced beer, no longer seemed as satisfying.

"You're in trouble, boy," Frank said, when Riley headed into the kitchen.

"Sorry, Frank. Time got away from me." He reached for the apron he'd left behind earlier. It now sat folded on an empty shelf in the kitchen. Stace's doing? Or Frank's?

Frank put a hand on Riley's arm. "Leave it. Come back tomorrow. When you're ready to work, not pretend to work." The rebuke sounded clear and strong.

"All I did was take a long lunch. I apologized." Riley had taken dozens of long lunches when he worked at McKenna Media. So many, in fact, they had become a running joke.

Apparently, none of this was funny to Frank. "What, do you think we're all sitting here twiddling our thumbs all day? You want a job, you work. Not let the rest of us pick up your slack."

The sandwich Riley had had at lunch sat heavy in his stomach. He glanced back at the diner, at Stace working hard, and the guilt that had been nothing more than a whisper earlier became a full-out scream in his head. What had he been thinking, leaving her to handle this alone? He'd run out of here, thinking only of himself, of shedding the responsibilities that had become a second coat. Not of her.

He knew how hard the job was. This entire week, he'd found little ways to get out of working too hard. Asking her to refill customers' drinks. Leaving her to do the cleanup. And now, leaving her to handle the afternoon alone. No wonder she'd shot him that glare. He deserved it—and more.

He thought of all those long lunches. They weren't the joke—he was. God, what an idiot he had been. A lazy, irresponsible idiot.

"I'm sorry."

"I'm not the one you need to apologize to." Frank pivoted to face Riley again. "You know, it's okay to admit you ain't got it all together. People respect a man who's honest with himself and with others."

Riley didn't reply. He just slipped the apron on and tied it behind his back.

"I've known you a long time, Riley." Frank dumped in several cupfuls of mayonnaise, then started mixing the coleslaw, the spatula digging deep in the oversized stainless steel bowl. "You've always taken your time like you didn't have any place to get to."

"My other job was…flexible."

"Or maybe it's more you didn't have any place you *wanted* to go." Frank finished the coleslaw, wrapped it in plastic wrap, then stowed it in the refrigerator. "Once you find where it is you want to go, I think you'll be more inclined to have some staying power." Then Frank turned away and headed for the sink to wash his hands.

Any place he wanted to go.

Was that why Riley had jumped from job to job? Heck, woman to woman? He'd spent his whole life…

Searching.

And what had he found? Nothing. Not a damned thing. What on earth was he looking for?

The answer didn't magically appear, so Riley headed out to the diner, grabbing the mop and rolling bucket on the way. Stace kept working, her back to him, even though she surely heard the clatter of the bucket's wheels as he approached. He stopped beside her. "I'm sorry."

"I'm not talking to you." She crossed to wipe off the next table.

"Stace, I'm sorry. I just got overwhelmed by the job and—"

She spun back. "You think I don't get overwhelmed? Or Frank doesn't? You don't think most of the people who work a job have days when they just want to run for the hills, or lie in bed, for the fun of it?"

"I'm sure you do. I'm not arguing that."

"No, but what you're doing is letting us down. I don't need another man who's going to let me down, Riley, so if this is your M.O., the door is right there." She turned back to the table, and wiped in furious circles.

"Why do you do that?"

"It's called cleaning up at the end of the day."

"I meant, why do you lump me in with every other man you know?"

"Because I've dated you. Not you, but your kind. Heck, I almost married a man just like you. Selfish, irresponsible, answering to no one but himself. I wasted so many years...too many years, hoping he'd change. And he never did." She pivoted toward him, the wet rag raised in her hands like a weapon. "Tell me, how are you different? Are you looking for marriage? For commitment? For anything more permanent than a tan?"

The words stung. Was that how she saw him? Or who he had been? "I'm not here to stay, if that's what you're asking. You and me and Frank all knew this job was a temporary thing. A means to an end. I've told you that."

"Well, I'd appreciate it if you would work hard while you're getting your 'means to an end.' Because the rest of us have lives and responsibilities that depend on you being here and doing your share."

Then it hit him. The appointment she'd made. Her request to leave early. The roof. Damn. She was right. He hadn't been thinking about anyone but himself. And now he was staring right at the results of that choice. "Stace, I forgot all about your appointment."

"It's fine. I'll get another one." But her voice trembled when she said it, and she had returned to her table wiping.

He felt like a jerk. Was this what he'd become? A man who let other people down just to have lunch with a friend?

He put a gentle hand on Stace's shoulder. "I really am sorry about today. Why don't you let me make it up to you?"

She stopped working and turned to assess him. "I don't need you to do anything other than just show up when you say you're going to."

"Deal." He shook with her, which brought a ghost of a smile to Stace's lips. "Did you have another roofer lined up?"

She sighed. "I haven't had time to find one. I made six calls, and this guy was the only one who called me back. I think reliable handymen are harder to find than unicorns."

"Or responsible playboys?"

She laughed, and it sounded like sunshine. "I heard those are an endangered species."

Riley chuckled, then realized how true that was, even if they were joking. He flipped out his cell phone and scrolled through the numbers. Then he pressed Send and put the phone to his ear.

"What are you doing?" she asked.

"Calling a roofer. One of the guys I went to high school with—"

"Don't." She put a hand over his. "I can take care of myself."

He leaned in toward her. "I have no doubt that you can. But this is all my fault, and I feel bad about leaving you in the lurch today, so please, let me help you. The least I can do is clean up the mess I made." He was getting involved again, and even as his mind screamed caution, his gut countered.

Her gaze assessed him, and she worried her bottom lip. He could see the struggle in her eyes, the tough decision on whether to accept his help or throw it back in his face. "If I let you do this, it's only because I don't want to spend any more time than necessary in your guest house."

"Agreed." By making this call, Riley ensured Stace's departure. There'd be no more pancakes on the counter, or floral bags in his bathroom. The thought saddened him, but before he could figure out why, the man on the other end answered. Riley explained the situation, then set up an appointment and ended the call. "He'll be out tonight. And he'll be fair on price."

"Thank you."

He chuckled. "That was hard for you, I know."

It took a moment, but then a smile filled her face. "What will be harder is you getting back into my good graces again if you're ever late, or let me down."

The trouble was, Riley knew that answer already. Some day, and probably soon, he would let her down. It was what he did, after all.

Stace woke up in Riley's guest bedroom on the second morning and told herself not to get too used to the feeling of the soft bed, luxurious linens, quiet grounds. But here she was again.

She had told Frank she'd be in late, so she could get Jeremy off to his first day of school okay. Riley had offered to cover, and Frank had called in Irene, the waitress who was on maternity leave. Stace glanced at the clock, and realized she hadn't slept this late in months, maybe years.

Then she glanced at the calendar and realized what day it was. Her heart lurched, and she took a moment to compose herself. Had she gotten so distracted in the past few days that she hadn't noticed the calendar?

Stace tugged on a robe and padded out to the kitchen. Jeremy was still asleep on the couch, looking so much like his mother that Stace's heart broke. She missed her sister with a pain that edged through her like a knife. "Where are you, Lisa?" Stace whispered to the walls. There was no answer, of course. There never was.

Almost her entire family, gone. Some days, the empty echoes on the family tree hit especially hard. Like today.

So Stace did what she always did. She busied herself with tasks that kept her mind from thinking too much. Putting some hard-boiled eggs on to boil, making coffee, then showering and dressing while waiting for the eggs to cook. When she was done, she woke Jeremy, and prodded the reluctant teenager toward the shower.

While she waited, Stace took the time to glance around Riley's home. She'd expected more of a bachelor pad, complete with overstuffed leather furniture, sports memorabilia, and a year's supply of unhealthy snacks. Riley's house was sedate, with tasteful decorations and comfortable furniture that beckoned guests. The rooms were tidy, the carpets clean, and the faint scent of chlorine from the nearby pool lingered in the air. Did Riley clean up after himself? Had he done the decorating? Or let someone else do it?

And why did she care? She'd meant what she'd said about not getting involved with him, or anyone for that matter, but especially him.

Hadn't he proven yesterday that he was unreliable? In the end, Riley McKenna would run from responsibility like it was a forest fire. She needed to remember that—and not get tempted by his lips, his eyes, his words. It had taken her heart a long time to recover from being broken by Jim, and she didn't want to go there again.

The problem? Every time Riley looked at her, she thought of what they had started—and not yet finished. What if she hadn't jumped out of the pool? What if she had kissed him?

The door opened, and Stace pivoted, to find Riley standing there, as if she'd conjured him up simply by thinking about him. He was wearing jeans and a Morning Glory Diner T-shirt that was sporting a ketchup stain on one side, a coffee stain on the other. She felt a smile rush to her face, along with a hot rush of tears. Riley, of course, couldn't know what today was, but just having him here filled her with gratitude. "I thought you were taking my shift," she said. "Why are you here?"

"Things slowed down enough for Irene to handle it. Frank told me, in his exact words, 'to get the hell out of here and make sure Jeremy gets his butt to school. And that Stace doesn't cry when he leaves.'"

Stace laughed. "That's Frank."

"And I thought that since I'd gone to that school, it might make things a little easier on Jeremy to have me along."

Who was Riley McKenna? Every time she thought he

was an insensitive, self-centered playboy, he went and did something like this. Something sweet. Something that caught her off guard, and tangled her heart. "Well, thank you."

"No problem." His gaze caught hers, and for a second she had the crazy thought that he was going to kiss her. That same rush of anticipation roared to life inside her, then dropped away when Riley cleared his throat. "I'm just going to go change. I'll be back."

Then he headed down the hall, and Stace returned to her breakfast. But the eggs had lost their flavor and she tossed them out uneaten.

For the first time in a month, Jeremy smiled. Stace wanted to hug her nephew, but held back, afraid of breaking whatever magic spell had come over him when he walked into the Wilmont Academy.

"This place is so cool, Riley," Jeremy said as he spun in a slow circle around the lobby outside the principal's office. "Did you see all the artwork on the walls?"

"Yep. It's everywhere. They have classes in film and photography, too. And dance, though I don't know if that's your style."

Jeremy laughed. Actually laughed. "Me? No way, man."

"It's a good way to get the ladies." Riley patted his chest. "You're looking at a graduate of Ballroom Dancing 101."

Beside them, Stace stifled a smirk. Riley, ballroom dancer? That she'd pay money to see.

Jeremy's nose wrinkled as if he'd just eaten a lemon. "Didn't it make you feel…girlie?"

"Not one bit." Riley stepped over, swung an arm around Stace's waist, then spun her to the right with two quick movements. He stopped, leaned over, and gave her a quick, breathless dip. She tried to hold back her laughter, but it bubbled up all the same. "Is that girlie?" Riley asked.

"Not one bit," Stace said. In fact it was every inch manly, and had awakened some very heated hormonal responses inside her body. If they hadn't been standing in the lobby of a school...

But they were. She scrambled out of his arms and back to a standing position before she got too used to the feeling of being held by him, or started daydreaming about being in his arms for a whole lot more than a simple dance.

A door to their right opened and a woman emerged. She was tall, slender, and had long dark hair that flowed down her back. One of those women so beautiful they made everything around them, even the handmade art decorating the walls, pale in comparison. "What shenanigans are you up to in my hall, Mr. McKenna?"

Riley grinned. "None at all, Miss Purcell."

She laughed, then placed a hand on his arm and leaned in close. "Too bad." Her voice was husky, sexy.

To Stace, the two of them seemed overly familiar, and she could read the undercurrent of a past relationship in the air. There was too much of a smile, too close of a touch. As Riley introduced her to Merry Purcell, Stace tried very hard not to hate the woman on the spot.

After all, it wasn't her fault that she'd reminded Stace of all the reasons why she shouldn't be involved with Riley. Of the ex-boyfriend who had broken her heart by running off with another woman.

So Stace put on a smile she didn't feel and waited until Jeremy had been introduced and then sent on his way to his first class. The gorgeous Miss Purcell got back to work, and Riley and Stace headed out the door.

"I appreciate you coming along," she said.

"Just wanted to be sure his first day went off without a hitch." Riley thumbed toward his car. "I'm heading back to work. Do you want me to drop you off at home?"

The responsibilities for today had dropped away, and as Stace took in the bright day around her, she was reminded again of the date. She could have gone back to the diner, but for now, she wanted to be alone.

How she wished her father had been here to see his grandson enrolled in this school. He would have been the first one to offer Jeremy a hearty congratulations, and the proudest relative in the parking lot. Stace's gaze went to the skies, to the dark gray clouds that hung over Boston, and maybe, hung over wherever her sister was now. Did Lisa even know what she had left behind? And would she ever come back?

Stace ached to talk to her father. He'd always had some little snippet of wisdom that could turn any situation better.

"Stace?" Riley's voice pulled her back to the present. "Do you want me to drop you off somewhere?"

"Uh...no. I'll see you later." She turned away, and started to head down the sidewalk toward the train station. Above her, the sky rumbled. It was going to rain. Again.

An apt weather report, Stace supposed, and buttoned her sweater against the increasing breeze. A second later, the red sports car sidled up beside her and the passenger window descended. "Come on, at least let me give you a ride back to the house," Riley said.

"I'm not going home." Home? When had Riley's guest house become home? She cursed the slip of the tongue, and blamed it on her mind being on other things. Not this irrational, growing need to have him around.

"Okay," Riley said. "Then where are you going?"

She let out a long breath. "Listen, I'm sure Frank is expecting you back. Just go to the diner and I'll talk to you later."

"It's only ten. I have an hour until we start gearing up for lunch. And Irene's there right now." Above them, the skies opened up and the rain began falling in a steady sheet, soaking through Stace's sweater, and plastering her hair against her head. "Come on, don't be stubborn. Get out of the rain, Stace."

"I…" The rain cut off her argument. As much as she'd like to be stubborn, as he'd said, and just head off on her own, the darn subway station was three blocks away and she wasn't wearing a coat. And to be honest…

She didn't want to be alone right now.

So she opened the door and slid inside the car, settling against the soft black leather seat. For a sports car, the interior was decidedly roomy and nice. Riley pulled away from the curb, and started heading down the street.

"Where to?"

"Cedar Grove Cemetery. I can give you directions. It's over on Adams—"

"I know where it is." A shadow dropped over Riley's face. "Why do you want to go there?"

"You don't have to take me. I'll take the train." She reached for the door handle. The last thing she wanted to do was explain everything to Riley. If she did, she'd be letting him into her heart, and she'd just vowed five minutes ago not to do that.

Riley reached over and put a hand on hers. "I don't mind, Stace. Really."

She readied a reason again why she could do this on her own, but stopped it. Riley had accused her of never asking for help. Maybe he had a point. Right now, she needed…something.

Company at least.

She glanced at his face and saw earnest concern there. For the hundredth time, she wondered who Riley McKenna really was. The man who'd dated more women than she could count, or this tender man who wouldn't let her walk in the rain?

So she gave Riley directions, and within minutes, they'd reached the cemetery. She directed him through the wrought-iron gates, past the fish pond and the stone chapel, down the winding main path, then down a second smaller road on the right. As they got deeper into the cemetery and closer to her destination, Stace could feel emotion bubbling up in her chest. "Stop here."

He glided to a stop. "Stace—"

"I'll be right back." She tugged on the door handle and barreled out of the car and into the rain. The water sluiced down her face, blurring her vision, but it didn't matter. She knew her destination by heart. She climbed the small grassy hill until she reached a granite marker embedded in the ground. Grass had grown up around the edges, creeping onto the small gray slab.

KETTERING was carved across the top in block letters. Below that, two names in a smaller font. Karen on the left and David on the right, along with the dates of their deaths. Rain pooled in the etched letters of her parents' names, bubbling over into tiny ponds.

A sob hitched in Stace's throat. The rain fell hard on her head, her back. Above her, storm clouds rumbled with discontent.

"Oh, Dad, I miss you." She barely remembered her

mother, who had died when Stace was little. Almost all her memories centered around the burly David Kettering, who had a kind word for every person he met, and a joke for every friend he made. He'd been her rock, and then he was gone, and she'd been doing her best to stay strong ever since, and felt like she was failing.

There was a sound beside her, then the rain stopped falling on her shoulders. She turned, to find Riley standing there with an umbrella opened over her head. She gave him a weak smile. "Thanks."

He gestured at the granite marker. "Your father?"

She nodded. "He died eight years ago today. The Morning Glory was his baby, his and Frank's."

"I knew that place was special to you for more than just a job."

She stared at the grave while the rain pattered on the umbrella like a thousand fingers. "God, I miss seeing him there. I've been at the Morning Glory since the day I was tall enough to sit at one of the counter stools. At first, my sister and I were just there after school so my dad didn't have to get a babysitter. We'd sit at the counter, and Frank would spoil us rotten with French fries and ice cream sundaes, and all the pancakes we could eat." She smiled at the memory, and could almost see herself back there again, fingers all sticky with syrup, belly sloshing with milk. "Then when we got older, we started helping out. Wiping the tables, sweeping the floor. My sister never really liked the work, but I stuck with it. By the time I was in high school, I was waitressing over the summer."

"And after college, working there full-time?"

"I didn't go to college." She bent down and traced the letters of her father's name, feeling for the thousandth time like she had let him down for not following the dreams he'd had for her. How many times had she sat at the kitchen table, discussing her dream of going to business school? Of making it big in the corporate world? Fate had had other plans for Stace and even though she wondered if she'd missed anything by skipping college, she knew her heart would never have been in the corporate world. It was right there in the Morning Glory.

"I didn't go to college, because…" She paused, her fingers catching the raindrops that pooled on the stone like tears. "My father was hit by a car outside the diner a month after I graduated high school. I went to work full-time at the Morning Glory and have been there ever since." She gave the stone a final touch, then rose. "It was a way of staying close to him. And helping Frank, who was just devastated when my dad died."

"Stace, I'm so sorry. That had to be really hard on you."

She shrugged, but the tears in her eyes belied the show of nonchalance. "I got through it. By doing what my dad did. I went to work, and took care of others." She let out a long breath. "My sister took his death so much harder than I did, and that's when she fell into drugs. She was a great single mom to Jeremy before that, but it was as if this was one more burden she couldn't carry. For a while she lived with me, then she'd disappear, come back, disappear again. Until she finally left for good last month and left me a note asking me to take care of Jeremy."

"Through all this," Riley said, "who took care of you?"

Stace turned away. This was why she rarely opened up to people. Because when she did, they asked the tough questions, the ones she avoided at all costs. "I am fine...as long as I'm working."

"And when you're not?"

Damn this man. He seemed to have a bead on the very things she didn't want to think about. "I'm always working," she said instead of the truth. That when she paused to think about how her life had been upended, and how she had put everything on hold—college, marriage, children—that it allowed regret to crawl in and make itself at home.

"Maybe it's time you did something other than work."

She shook her head and started heading down the hill. There was no solace to be found here today. No voice of wisdom, no comforting hugs. Just a cold, wet stone. "You don't understand, Riley. I can't. The Morning Glory was my dad's business, and it needs me to be plugged in, to keep it running. Especially now that it's struggling. Frank can't do it on his own."

"No one said he had to. But the job doesn't all have to fall on your shoulders."

They had reached the path beside his car. She wanted to just get in the car and drive away, and not have this conversation, but it was Riley's car and he had the keys, and he wasn't making any move to leave. "Stop trying to question my life and my choices, Riley."

"I'm not. I'm just telling you there are other options."

"Like what? Living off my family? Because unlike you, I don't have one that has scholarships and guest houses at their disposal. There's me, and that's it. If I don't go to work, I don't eat." She saw that her words had hit close to home, and she reached out a hand to him. Her mouth had gotten away from her and regret filled her. "I'm sorry. I shouldn't have said that."

"No, you're right." He brushed a tendril of wet hair

off her forehead. "If there's one thing I've learned in the few days I've worked at the Morning Glory, it's that you have to work hard for what you want. I've gotten by for too many years on the bare minimum. And I don't want to do that anymore."

She let out a little laugh. "Well, I wouldn't mind a few days of the bare minimum."

A grin curved across his face. "Maybe we can work out a compromise. I had some ideas to increase business. I'd love to run them by you."

"Okay." She echoed his smile for a moment. "When I'm working at the diner, sometimes I really miss my dad. He made every day there one to look forward to."

"He sounds like he was a wonderful guy."

"He was." The smile hurt her face now, and tears threatened the back of her eyes. The rain kept up its steady patter, as if urging her to cry with it. She had been strong for so long, never showing an emotion, just putting in the hours at work, and lately, helping to raise Jeremy. Before that, it had been taking care of her sister, being the one that Lisa turned to when she was lost or cold or hungry. In all that time, Stace had put her own needs on hold. And now here was Riley, the one man she kept trying to resist, standing in the rain with an umbrella and an understanding smile, and in the process, opening her heart a little at a time. She swiped at her face and looked back at the hill that held her father's grave. "I wanted to come here today to tell him about Jeremy getting into that school. My dad would be so proud." She rolled her eyes and wiped away a tear. "It's silly. I mean, he's not even there. But I still like to talk to him."

"Aw, Stace." Riley put an arm around her shoulders

and drew her against his chest. He was warm and hard and smelled like soap. "It's not silly at all. Not one bit."

She looked up into his gentle blue eyes, and in them, saw a mirror of her own sorrow there, a peek inside the depths of Riley. For a long while, neither of them said a word. The rain pattered on the sidewalk, while Riley held onto Stace, and Stace held onto Riley.

"I come here a lot, too," he said softly. "My parents are buried just over the hill. For me, it's been twenty years since they died, but there are times when it feels like yesterday. And you know, all the scholarships and guest houses in the world don't make up for that."

"No, they don't." She'd never have expected that Riley, of all people, would understand. Would empathize. "I'm sorry I said that stuff about money."

"It's okay. If it had been me, I probably would have said the same thing." He sighed. "I come here sometimes for answers," he said. "But they aren't here, are they?"

She shook her head. "No. I sure wish they were." A long, shuddering breath escaped her.

Then she gave up the fight and leaned the rest of the way into Riley, pouring her tears into his soft shirt, and her grief into his broad shoulders. He just held her, his chin resting gently on the top of her head, and the umbrella shielding them both from the storm. She told herself not to get so close, not to care so much. But she did, oh, how she did.

After a long while, the rain began to ease and Stace's tears dried up. Riley pulled back. "You okay now?"

She nodded. "Thank you. I'm sorry for—"

He pressed a finger to her lips. "Don't. Don't ever apologize for needing someone."

"I don't…" She shook her head. He was right. "Okay, I won't. Thank you, Riley."

"You're welcome. Anytime." His hand slid down and cupped her jaw, turning her face up to meet his. His blue eyes were soft, caring, yet filled with as many mysteries as the stormy skies above. "I have never met a woman like you."

She shrugged. "I'm a waitress from Dorchester, Riley. I'm nothing special."

"Oh, you are wrong, Stace. Very, very wrong." He leaned down until his gaze was riveted on hers, and the only thing she could hear was the rapid beat of her own heart. He tipped the umbrella away from them, letting it fall to the ground. The rain had slowed to a mist, and it dusted them both with a soft blanket of wet.

Time slowed. The world stopped. And then Riley McKenna leaned in and captured Stace's mouth with his.

He kissed her tenderly at first, a long, slow caress across her lips that seemed almost reverent. Two kindred souls, seeking comfort, solace, connection. She leaned into him, and the kiss deepened, became a concert of sensations on her mouth. She closed her eyes, and for the first time in forever, allowed herself to do nothing but feel. Feel Riley's firm body against hers. Feel Riley's strong palm on her jaw. Feel Riley's lips moving against hers, his tongue dancing with hers.

And most of all, feel Riley McKenna becoming an indelible part of her heart.

CHAPTER EIGHT

RILEY had not intended to kiss Stace Kettering. To do anything other than offer her comfort, a shoulder to lean on. But then she had looked up at him with those sad eyes and that sweet smile, and he'd wanted nothing more than to make her his.

That was a dangerous thing. He was beginning to crave her presence, to think about her all the time and to wonder about what would happen next. It was as if he was falling for her, and that was one thing he couldn't do. She deserved a man who wanted to settle down in that little house in Dorchester, patch her roof, and fix her plumbing. Not a man who had all the sticking power of wet glue. He'd always excelled at short-term relationships because they were a hell of a lot safer than the kind where a man settled down for the rest of his life. Did he need a bigger reminder of why, than he had right here, standing in this cemetery?

Nothing lasted. And pretending otherwise only led to pain.

So he had pulled away, even as a large part of him didn't want to let go. He knew better, though, and knew deep inside he wasn't interested in the white picket fence life.

They both opted to go back to the diner, and relieve

the harried Irene, who thanked them up and down for letting her go home early. "The baby isn't letting me sleep yet," Irene said. "If I'm lucky, I can get a nap in before she needs to eat again."

After Irene was gone, and it was just Riley and Stace in the front of the diner again, the reality became clear to Riley. More dishes, more customers, more orders to take and fill. The prospect suffocated him, and he chafed at the thought of putting in several more hours here.

Because they'd gotten close earlier, and that had knocked him off-kilter again? It was like a push-pull in his chest. Every time expectations were heaped on Riley, all he wanted to do was...

Escape.

Riley McKenna didn't get close. Didn't form long-term relationships. Didn't do anything other than find one more way to amuse himself. That's what he needed to focus on, instead of his mind circling back to one tender moment in the rain.

The rest of the day's shift passed quickly. Stace left early to meet Jeremy outside the school, and Riley followed once the cleanup was done, to gather them from the train station and drive them back to the guest house. It was all beginning to feel a lot like...

A family.

So ordinary. Like peanut butter and jelly sandwiches.

Jeremy talked nonstop the whole way home about his day at school, and as soon as they got in the door, he started in on his first homework project, spreading out paper, pencils, and paints on the kitchen table.

"Is it okay if I use the pool?" Stace asked.

"Sure. Make yourself at home." He thought of offering to go with her, but then remembered the last time he had done that. Seeing her in her swimsuit, feeling her slick, wet body against his—

He'd be right back to doing what he swore he wouldn't do again. Kissing her.

Stace changed, then headed out to the pool. Riley stayed in the kitchen, loading dishes into the dishwasher—it was amazing how domesticated he'd been forced to become now that he wasn't paying for a maid service—and watching Stace from the kitchen window. She sliced through the water with a pro's precision, in long, easy, slow strokes that barely made a splash.

His phone rang. He glanced at the caller ID and for a second, considered letting the call go to voice mail. Instead, he answered it. "Hey, Alec."

"Are you sick? Dead? What the hell are you doing home, Riley? It's Friday night."

He hadn't even realized it was the weekend already. That alone showed how much Stace had gotten to him. Riley forced out a chuckle. "I'm just letting you guys get a head start."

"Oh. We have a head start, and then some." Alec laughed. "We're down at Flanagan's. I'll hold a seat for you."

Riley glanced at Jeremy, doing homework at the kitchen table, while nibbling from a plate of cookies from the diner that was sitting beside a cold glass of milk. A homey, cozy, suffocating scene.

"Give me twenty." Riley hung up, then headed into the shower. In a few minutes he was ready. He grabbed his car keys from the table. "Tell your aunt I went out for a while."

Jeremy arched a brow. "You go out a lot."

"No, I don't."

The teenager shrugged and went back to drawing. "Whatever. I'll tell Aunt Stace."

Riley leaned against the counter. "Does she go out a lot?"

"Aunt Stace? Heck, no." Jeremy scoffed. "She has, like, zero life. When I get old, I'm not going to be like that."

"Doesn't she date?"

"If you can call it that." Jeremy put down his pencil. "The last guy Aunt Stace went out with said he'd take her out to dinner. He showed up on her doorstep with a pizza and a six-pack."

"Oh, that's lame." Riley had a lot of other adjectives in mind, but he kept them to himself. No wonder Stace was gun-shy.

"Yeah. I felt really bad for her," Jeremy said. "I wasn't living there then but Aunt Stace told my mom about it." Jeremy's gaze went to a space in the distance. "Aunt Stace used to come over a lot to kinda check on my mom and me. Then when my mom started…being gone a lot, I just started staying at Aunt Stace's. And then one day my mom dropped off all my stuff, and she left, and I stayed behind."

Riley's heart went out to the boy. Riley's parents had died, not abandoned him. It was a car accident, not a choice, that took them out of his life. "That had to be tough on you."

"It is what it is, whether I like it or not." Jeremy shrugged but the pain still shone in his eyes and the hunch of his shoulders. "My aunt is pretty cool, I guess. Sometimes I feel bad about giving her a hard time."

"It's hard to grow up so fast."

The boy doodled on a scrap of paper. "Yeah."

Riley dropped into the chair beside Jeremy. "When

I went to live with my grandparents, I gave them a hard time, too. I guess I blamed them for what happened to my parents, even though it wasn't their fault. I wanted to be mad at somebody, because I felt robbed."

"I guess I did the same thing." Jeremy toyed with the pencils, rolling red over green, over yellow, over purple. "I still miss my mom."

"I hope she's back soon."

Jeremy shrugged as if he didn't care. Red went over green, over yellow, over purple, again and again. "Hey, uh, Riley, can I ask you something?"

"Sure."

"It's, uh, about girls. And I don't want to ask my aunt. You know it's like…"

"A guy thing."

"Yeah."

"Well, you've asked the right person. Girls are my specialty." Even as he joked about it, Riley sent up a silent prayer that whatever the boy asked him, he'd dispense good advice. He'd never been a father figure, in any sense of the word, to anyone, and the thought that Jeremy already looked at him as someone he could go to for advice both pleased and terrified Riley. "So, uh, what do you want to know?"

"There was this girl in my class today." A red blush filled Jeremy's cheeks. "She's, like, into art, too, although her stuff is more deco. She's really good, too, but she kept asking me what I thought. Like, if she should use a charcoal or an HB pencil, if she should color this part red or orange. I didn't know if she really didn't know or if she…well…you know."

"Liked you."

A shy smile curved across Jeremy's face. "Yeah."

Riley grinned. He remembered those days when he'd

first noticed girls. How he'd worked so hard to impress little Amanda Wilson in his seventh-grade English class. He'd stammered and blubbered and struck out. Time and experience had taken him from that awkward stage to one with slightly more finesse. "If a girl keeps asking for your help with a problem she can solve herself, chances are she likes you."

What did it say when a woman *refused* his help over and over again? Riley glanced at the glass doors. All he saw of Stace was the flash of her arm—up, down, up, down, like a piston.

"You think she likes me?" Jeremy asked.

"Definitely."

The shy smile on Jeremy's face morphed into a beam. "Cool. Maybe I'll send her an email or something tonight."

"Just take it slow, Jeremy. Don't rush into—"

But the boy was already gone, off to the computer in the corner of the living room. Riley got to his feet and turned toward the door, then pivoted back. Stace was still slicing through the water in controlled, even movements. Alone, in control, and so typical of Stace. She gave off the impression that she was an island unto herself, but Riley suspected it was all a cover.

He thought about what Jeremy had told him, and decided Alec could wait another night. Stace Kettering deserved a night out. And if anyone knew how to romance a woman on a date, it was Riley McKenna.

He just had to be smart enough to take his own advice and not rush into anything. No matter how tempting the race might be.

"How fast can you get dressed?"

At the same time Stace had come up for air, she'd

heard the door open. She stopped swimming, shook the water out of her ears, and stared up at Riley. "What did you say?"

"How fast can you get dressed?" Riley asked. He looked impossibly tall standing above her on the pool's edge, and impossibly sexy in a pair of jeans and a black button-down shirt. His hair was dark and wet from the shower, punctuating the blue in his eyes.

She stood up in the shallow end of the pool. Water cascaded down her back, over her face. She swiped it away with her palm and brushed her hair out of her eyes. "Uh, I don't know." She paused, caught her breath. "A half hour?"

"How about twenty?"

"What am I getting dressed for?"

"A date. In the city. With me."

Stace shook her head. "Riley, I'm just going to go to bed early and—"

"The diner opens two hours later on Saturday mornings, so you can go out tonight. And besides, I think you deserve a night out. One where the guy treats you to more than a six-pack and a pizza in your own living room."

She laughed. "You've been talking to Jeremy."

"As a matter of fact, I have. He asked me for some advice, and I gave it to him."

"You?" Stace cringed. Riley giving advice to her nephew? She wasn't sure she liked that. At all. "About what?"

"Women. And don't worry, I ended with the words 'take it slow.'"

She breathed a sigh of relief. "Good."

The advice surprised her, too. She'd thought Riley was all man's man, the kind of guy who would kid another about dating widely, and encourage her nephew to do the same. Dispensing the whole "don't get roped into marriage ever" talk. But he'd handled it well, from what he'd said, and she appreciated that. If there was one thing Jeremy needed, it was a steady male influence.

Riley surprised her every time she turned around, both with the way he'd handled Jeremy and the impromptu date. That both intrigued her—and scared her—because this Riley, the one who surprised her, was someone she was starting to like. A lot.

He held out a towel to her. "So come on, let's go out tonight." She hesitated. "I promise, I'll take it slow, too."

She tried to hold it back, but a laugh escaped her all the same. "Okay, you convinced me." She placed her hands on either side of the pool ledge and hoisted herself out. Riley wrapped her in the towel, and paused, just a moment longer than necessary. His hands wrapped around her arms with gentle strength, and his body provided the hint of heat behind her. She glanced over her shoulder. "Thanks."

"Anytime," he said, and she knew he wasn't talking about towels.

She swallowed. Did she want more than this? Or did she want to maintain the status quo, stay coworkers, and nothing more?

"I, ah, better get ready," she said.

"Okay." He released her, then stepped forward to hold the door as they headed back to the guest house. The cool night air made Stace shiver. Or maybe it was the anticipation of a date—a real date—with a handsome man. How long had it been since she'd been out on the town? So long, she couldn't even remember the last time.

Twenty minutes later, Stace had showered and

changed. She didn't have much to choose from for clothes, just a few things she had hurriedly thrown into a bag before she left the Dorchester house. Thankfully, one of the items was a short dark brown jersey dress that always looked good and never wrinkled, sort of her standby outfit for any occasion—party, date, church. She paired it with the lone set of heels that had been hanging on the hook with the dress—nothing special, just some strappy black heels she'd bought on sale a couple years ago. She took time drying her hair, getting it smooth and straight, then spent a few extra minutes on her makeup, telling herself it was just because she was excited to be going out.

Not to impress Riley McKenna. At all.

When she came out of the bathroom, Riley looked up from the newspaper he was reading and let out a low whistle. "You look amazing."

She smoothed a hand down the soft fabric of the dress. "It is a little prettier than the Morning Glory Diner T-shirt."

"Oh, I think you look pretty hot in that, too." He grinned, then rose. "Are you ready?"

"Where's Jeremy?" She'd been in such a rush to get ready, she hadn't even thought about leaving her nephew home alone. Granted, he was old enough to handle it, but still, she worried.

"I sent him over to the main house," Riley said. "He wanted to show my grandmother what he was working on for school, and she needed some company, even if she won't admit it. She's got the dog, but she likes human companionship. And I think Jeremy wanted to spoil Heidi while he was over there."

She was touched that Riley had thought of something to keep Jeremy busy—and in the process, given him a babysitter of sorts, one who clearly held a soft spot in Riley's heart. "You really watch out for her, don't you?"

He shrugged, as if it was no big deal. "She did it for me when I needed someone."

"Why Riley McKenna, you sound positively dependable. Not at all like your public image."

"I have a public image?"

"Yep." She tossed him as a smile as they walked out the door and down the walkway to the car. "Charming playboy, with nary a care in the world, is how I believe they characterized you in the gossip columns. Though the reporters might need to come up with some new adjectives. Like…good with a coffeepot, never disappoints on the fries and always…"

He paused in opening her door. "And always what?"

The dark night wrapped around them, and the quiet grounds left them in solitude. It was intimate, cozy, sexy. "Always…leaves them wanting to come back." The words escaped her in a soft rush.

Did she mean the diner?

Or herself?

He leaned in to her, and she caught her breath. Oh, what was she doing? She kept forgetting that she didn't want to get involved with him. Then he'd make her laugh or turn that irresistible grin on her, and Stace would fall for him all over again and forget her vow to not get too close.

"And how about you? Do you want to come back?" he asked, his voice as dark and intimate as the night.

Yes, she wanted to say, but instead she gave his chest a light jab, inserting distance between them. "I want my promised night on the town."

"Well, I'd hate to disappoint you." He pressed a quick kiss to her lips, which sent her heart racing all over again, and had her craving something more, something deeper, something…

Lasting.

But then she remembered that *lasting* and *permanent* were not adjectives used to describe Riley. He'd made that very clear, over and over again, and just because he was close to his grandmother or been nice to Jeremy didn't change anything. She'd do well to enjoy this night out, and take it as just that—a night out. Nothing more.

Nothing that would last longer than tonight.

They drove through the city, with its twinkling white lights and exclamation points of red taillights. Boston hummed with life, as busy at night as it was during the day. Riley had put down the windows, and Stace soaked up the sights, sounds, and smells. She had worked in this city forever, but never really experienced it, and barely ever at night. Getting up for work at four in the morning had put a serious crimp in her nightlife.

They stopped at a nightclub, where a valet came out for Riley's car. Riley greeted the man by name, then pressed a few bills into the man's hand. "Be nice to my car, Jimmy."

"I always am, Riley," the valet said with a grin, then he pulled away from the curb. The doorman pulled the door open for them, also greeting Riley by name, then the hostess, who led Riley to a table deep inside the club.

Stace sat down across from him, while the music pounded and pulsed around them and a rainbow of lights flickered across the dark room. The club was filled with bodies—a crush of people dancing, talking, laughing. She tapped her foot, and shifted her weight to the beat.

"You want to dance?"

"Oh, I'm not very good."

"You are. I've seen you, remember?" He rose and

waited for her to take his hand, then when she did, he led her to the dance floor. The music pounded, while Riley twirled her to the left. She stepped quickly with him, then stepped back when he moved forward.

She let the music sweep over her, like the water in the pool, until all she heard was the beat, all she felt was Riley's touch, all she knew was the movement of her own body. Inch by inch, she relaxed and allowed herself to let go, to forget everything in her life except this moment. Riley's smile widened, and he closed the gap between them, until her hips were shimmying against his pelvis, and the world became the two of them. The heat increased between them, the beat seemed to hasten, and Stace became very, very aware of every inch of Riley's body. About how it felt to touch him, be held by him, be close to him. Then the song ended, and they broke apart, as if someone had turned off a switch.

She stepped off the dance floor and Riley followed. "That was fun," she said.

"I'm glad you enjoyed it."

"I did." The song shifted again, and Stace itched to return to the floor. To his arms. Instead, she nodded toward the bar. The club had filled with even more people, until it was standing room only. "How about a drink?"

"How about we go someplace quieter? It's too crowded now."

A few minutes later, they were outside on the sidewalk, waiting for the valet to return with the car. Riley glanced back at the nightclub. People streamed in and out of the front door, like a tide ebbing and flowing on the beach. "You know, I used to really enjoy that place. But it's funny. I don't so much anymore."

"Why?" He was still holding her hand, and she realized she liked that. Too much.

"Guess my tastes are changing," Riley said. "Anyway, there's another club over on Boylston I like to hit, and there's always a party down in Southie. We could—"

"Riley..." She put a hand on his arm. "You don't need to impress me with clubs and valets and fancy drinks for us to have a nice time out. We can do something else."

"I'm not doing that. I'm..." He gave her a grin. "Okay, maybe I am. And I'm sorry it's not the Ritz or something like that. If I could have afforded it, I'd have taken you to the Top of the Hub."

"I don't need the Top of the Hub." He really didn't know her, did he? Or was it that Riley, a man who kept on going to places he didn't even like, didn't know himself that well, either? "You can have a lot of fun for free, or nearly free in this city."

The valet brought up their car. Riley tipped him, then held Stace's door before he slid into the driver's seat. "Where to now?"

"Do you trust me?"

His gaze held hers for a long, hot moment. The world dropped away, and the busy space closed in to be just the two of them. "Yes."

A delicious shiver chased down her spine, every time Riley looked at her in that intent, soul-seeking way. It was as if he could see inside her, see everything that she was thinking.

Did he know how much she wanted him to kiss her? How she melted every time he smiled? How she used to think she had it all together, in control, and had realized that with just one look, Riley McKenna could turn all that control upside down?

Yeah, it was probably a good thing he wasn't a mind reader.

She cleared her throat, and gestured toward the road. "Then let's head for Rowes Wharf. And I'll show you *my* definition of a good time, Riley."

CHAPTER NINE

RILEY had never been in a position like this. The roles reversed, with the woman planning the date. He had to admit, he kind of liked it.

They parked in a city garage, then headed up to the sidewalk. Stace turned to Riley, a knowing smile on her face. She had something planned, but what it was, he couldn't tell. "Can you wait here a second?" she asked. "I'll be right back." She dashed into a market beside them, and returned a few minutes later, holding a paper bag emblazoned with the market's name.

"What'd you buy?"

"That is a surprise. For me to know, and you to discover." A grin curved across her face. She was teasing him, and he liked it, very much. This was another side to Stace, something light and fun. He'd loved seeing that back in the club, watching her loosen up, pry off the bonds of her life. It was as if being away from the diner and her nephew had given her permission to peel back a layer of herself for him to see. Every moment he spent with Stace showed him another dimension.

"Let me carry the bag for you. I promise not to peek." He held up three fingers. "Scouts' honor."

"If you do—" she wagged a finger at him "—there will be dire consequences."

"Dire? What kind of dire? Hmm…almost makes me want to peek."

"Don't you dare." She laughed, then folded down the top of the bag and handed it to him. They walked down a brick pathway that ran alongside Rowes Wharf. Boats bobbed quietly in the water, and people strolled back and forth, enjoying the ocean breezes. The entire atmosphere offered a peaceful comfort, far removed from the city, even as traffic buzzed along a little way away.

And it was as far from what Riley normally did on a Friday night as one could get. He watched one of the boats pull away from the dock, embarking on a harbor dinner cruise. "If this was an ordinary date," he said to her, "I'd take you onto one of those boats and we'd have dinner out on the water. A waiter at our beck and call, and an unlimited supply of wine." He paused and turned to her. "I really did have plans to show you an incredible night on the town, or at least as incredible as I can get on my budget."

She stopped walking, cocked her head and studied him. "Maybe that's the problem."

"What? My lack of funds? I agree, but—"

"No, not that. You doing what you normally do." She shrugged. "I saw you back at the club. You didn't look happy."

A couple of lovebirds strolled past them, giggling into each other's faces and holding on so tight, it seemed they were one, not two. For a second, Riley envied their obvious love for each other. Then he looked away and the feeling was gone.

"Well, that's because it was loud and busy and…" He let out a breath, and finally faced what had been bothering him back at the club. The club scene no longer fit him. For years, it had been the only place he'd gone, but now, with Stace, he realized it wasn't what he wanted anymore. "I've gone there a hundred times over the years, but you know, I guess I never realized how much I didn't enjoy it."

"Then why do you go?"

"Because that's what us playboys do." He gave her a grin.

But in that smile, Stace detected something she had rarely seen in Riley. Vulnerability. She wondered what he was hiding, keeping to himself. There was something there, she'd bet a month's pay on it. Yet Riley had yet to fully open up to her. He kept retreating behind that grin.

"True," she said. "But is it what former playboys turned waiters at diners do?"

"Maybe not. It's expensive to go out like that." His gaze, and even though the night was dark and the lights were dim, she could see the connection in those blue depths. It made her shiver with anticipation.

"Then maybe learning to live on a server's salary will teach you a thing or two." She gestured to a bench that sat along the waterfront. Few people had ventured this far down the dock, and they had the space mostly to themselves. "Like how to have a romantic date on a budget."

He waved an arm toward the bench. "After you, madam."

She laughed, then settled on one end, and he settled on the other, with the bag between them. The stars glowed steady in the sky above them, punctuated by the occasional moving light of a departing or landing plane. The water lapped gently against the pier, sloshing up the dock posts, then down along the sides of the boats moored nearby. Far in the distance, the sound of boat engines purred on the water, while the muted steady song of highway traffic sang behind them.

"A small budget does force you to be creative. That's something I haven't been in a long time." His gaze went out to the water. "I guess that's what I really need to do—put my creativity to work. Like at the diner."

"You're going to start concocting recipes now?"

He laughed. "No. Just a marketing campaign to increase business. I think you need an event. Something that will get people talking about the Morning Glory."

"That'd be nice. But those kinds of things take time to plan. And getting exposure in such a big city is tough."

She had a point. He needed to mull this over some more. He didn't want to just throw out an idea just to say something. "We'll think of something."

"And until then, let's have dinner." She reached into the bag. "Date element number one. Wine." She handed him a bottle of white wine, followed by a set of plastic cups to drink from. "Date element number two. Cheese."

He laughed at the package of sliced cheese. It was a variety of flavors, in different hues of yellow and white. "Looks good so far."

"Date element number three. Bread." She tugged out a loaf of bread. The fresh-baked scent filled the space between them. "Date element number four. Grapes."

He held up the wine. "I thought we had plenty of them in here."

"We do, but we can always use more." A teasing smile played on her lips, lit the green in her eyes. "And finally, date element number five. Lots of napkins." She pulled out a stack of paper napkins and plopped them on the bench, then stowed the bag underneath.

"You've thought of everything. I'm impressed."

"It's just wine and cheese. Nothing big."

But to Riley it was. Not because of the beautiful setting of the Boston Harbor Hotel's famed lighted archway behind them. Or the quiet solitude of the oceanfront. Or the mild, cloudless night that dotted the sky with stars.

It was Stace Kettering. The way she had adapted easily to their two vastly different dates and made a nighttime picnic on Rowes Wharf seem like the most romantic place she'd ever been. On the water beside them, boats sliced through the water with blinking red and green lights, while couples strolled the pier arm in arm. Quiet, romantic.

Perfect.

And light years more romantic than anything he'd ever done on a date. There was no hovering waiter, no softly playing instrumental music, no perfectly appointed dining room. It was simple, and nice. Nothing extra, nothing unnecessary.

It was as if Stace had read his mind, and given him something he didn't even know he wanted. Until he had it.

Stace gestured toward the wine. "Why don't you open that?"

He held up a finger. "Oh, you forgot one thing. A corkscrew."

Stace laughed. "We're dining on a server's salary, remember? That's a screw-top wine bottle."

He chuckled, then opened the bottle of Chardonnay and poured them each some. Stace unwrapped the cheese and bread, then held the loaf toward him. "Tear off a hunk, pair it with some cheese. It's Bohemian and—" She moaned in anticipation, and he wanted to grab her right then, and taste her, not the food, but then she smiled and the moment was gone. "And oh, so delicious that way."

He did as she instructed, and watched her do the same. The combination was a culinary delight, soft cheddar cheese melting on his tongue, with the rustic notes of the bread. He raised his plastic cup to hers. "To inventive dates."

"And flexible boyfriends." She clicked her glass against his, then sipped.

Riley shifted on the bench, a little closer to her. "Is that what I am? Your boyfriend?"

"Well, no, I didn't mean that. I was just being clever." She looked away, and the night hid whether she was embarrassed, or avoiding the subject.

"Why do you do that?" Riley asked.

"Do what?"

"Push me away every time I try to get close?"

She looked at him, green eyes wide, inquisitive. "Why do you try so hard to get close?"

"Touché." He had to admit, Stace Kettering was a woman who gave as good as she got. She was different from anyone he'd ever met before. Because she was...

Challenging.

Yes, that was the word. She challenged him, in a hundred different ways. To act better, to be more, and most of all, to be as honest with her as he wanted her to be with him.

He had dated dozens of women, but none had made him want to try so hard, to work so much to impress her, charm her.

Win her heart.

Why do you try so hard to get close?

He propped one ankle over the opposite knee, and leaned back on the bench. He didn't sip at the wine, didn't eat the food, just watched the dark arrowed shadows of boats making their way through the harbor. "I've never really been close to anyone. Or let anyone get that close to me."

One sentence, and it was probably the most honest one Riley McKenna had ever spoken in his whole life. He didn't know if it was the setting, or the woman beside him, or the wine, which he'd only had a sip of, but something made him want to open up, just a little.

"Why not?" Stace asked, her voice a quiet melody. Challenging him again, to open up even more.

He hesitated, but then realized that all that holding back, keeping himself to himself, had gotten him nowhere but in loud nightclubs with people he barely knew, and dates that had all the depth of a puddle. He used to think he enjoyed all that, because it put no ties on him, but in the last few weeks, he'd realized that lack of ties left him with a feeling of emptiness.

He'd perfected the art of avoiding heavy subjects, and now, it seemed like every one of those subjects he had avoided were weighing on his shoulders. What would it be like to lessen that load?

He'd done it already, in little steps, with Stace at her house, then in the pool, and finally, at the cemetery. In the process, he had started to find new dimensions to himself. Some he liked. Some he didn't. It was as if he was a pen-and-ink drawing and the closer he got to Stace, the more he added color and layers to that image.

"I guess that fear comes from losing my parents when I was so young," Riley said after a moment. "That kind of loss rocks your world in a way nothing else ever does."

She nodded. "I know what you mean. It leaves you—" she let out a breath "—vulnerable. I mean, I know I'm a grown-up now and I should be able to take care of myself, and I do, but when your parents are gone, it's like all of a sudden, the people who are supposed to watch out for you and warn you not to cross the street without looking aren't there."

He hadn't thought of it that way. He'd had his grandparents, and his older brothers, and there'd been advice aplenty from all of them. But none of them, no matter how much they loved him, had been his mother and father. "You're right. You can have all the surrogate parents in the world, but losing your own…it's different."

"We're orphans."

He let out a little laugh. "I'm a little old to be adopted."

"Me, too."

He drew her into him, his arm going around her shoulders. Riley bent to nuzzle a kiss into the top of her head. "Then I'll adopt you, Stace Kettering."

"You will?" She tossed him a grin. "I can be a handful."

"Me, too."

She curved into him, holding him as tight as he held her. "Then we'll adopt each other."

He let those words wash over him, and kept on holding her close. It was a fun fantasy to indulge, both of them needing someone else, and offering to be that for the other. "Will you read me stories at night?"

"I'm not very good at that. I put myself to sleep."

Riley laughed. "My father was like that. He worked really hard during the day, and my mom, who had had enough of three mischievous boys, always made my father do bedtime duty. He'd send the older two off to their room, then come see me. I was little, and always begging him for a story or two."

"What kind of stories?" Stace asked.

She was snuggled up against him, the food forgotten, the world a distant presence. It was nice…awfully nice.

"Adventure ones," Riley went on. "Like *Robinson Crusoe* and *The Swiss Family Robinson.* I liked anything where there was danger and weapons." He chuckled. "Typical boy, I guess."

"Jeremy was like that, too, when he was little. We worked our way through all the Hardy Boy mysteries one year. My sister was living with me, and I would read to Jeremy at night to get him to sleep."

"But did you ever fall asleep in the middle of the good parts?"

She thought for a second. "I don't think so."

"My dad did, all the time." Riley chuckled. "It didn't matter if the hero was about to be shot or the heroine was just kidnapped by train robbers. Dad would fall asleep at the point where I was on the edge of my seat with suspense. Drove me crazy. I couldn't wait for him to get home the next day and finish."

"Maybe he had an ulterior motive."

"Like what?"

"Maybe he wanted you to miss him. And be excited when he got home."

Riley considered that. Even though it had been over twenty years, he could remember his father walking through the door, and the three McKenna boys plowing into his chest, each clamoring for his attention. "We all hung on him like monkeys in a tree. He'd walk to the kitchen, with one or all of us hanging off his legs and arms."

She laughed. "I can picture that."

"But I was the youngest, the baby, you know, and he always propped me up on his arm. I think that made Finn and Brody jealous, but my dad said it was because they would have trampled me if he left me down on the floor." Riley smiled, and suddenly, the loss of his father and mother seemed to wash over him in a wave. Riley leaned forward, bracing his arms on his knees, and inhaled the salty tang of ocean air. "I...I wish he was still here."

Stace's hand went to his back. She rubbed gently, a comforting touch that told him she, of all the women in the world, understood. "I'm sorry, Riley."

He drew himself up, and her hand dropped away. "Yeah, me, too." He gathered the food and began to put it in the bag. "It's getting cold. Maybe we should get going."

"Uh...okay." She helped him pick up the rest of their meal. Riley tucked the bag under his arm, and they headed back up the dock and toward the car.

A part of him wanted to explain why he'd ended the conversation so fast, but the other part of him, the part that had won time and time again when it came to getting close to people, threw up the caution flag. Better to stay uninvolved, unattached, than to latch on to Stace and end up alone in the end. She was a woman who would see his opening up to her as commitment.

Yet, when he looked over at her as they drove back to his house, he wondered what it would be like to be committed to a woman like her. To know that she would be there, at the end of every single day, to greet him, hug him, kiss him.

Would every day be as sweet and delicious as that time on the pier? Or would he have a good time for a while, and then see it all taken away in the blink of an eye?

The ride passed quickly, and too soon, they pulled into the driveway of the guest house. The date was over.

A stone of disappointment sank in Riley's gut. "We're back."

"Yeah," she said.

"Do you, uh, want to go over and get Jeremy with me?"

"Sure. I want to thank your grandmother again, too."

Riley came around, opened her door, and waited for Stace to get out. When she rose, she brushed against him. The dark, quiet night wrapped around them like a cocoon and suddenly he didn't want the date to end. Didn't want them to go back to being coworkers. He wanted just a little bit more. Just tonight.

Riley wrapped an arm around her waist, and she shifted against him, let out a soft, enticing mew. Her chin went up, her green eyes met his, and everything inside him began to roar.

What was it about her that made him forget everything whenever she was in his arms? "I had a really nice time tonight," he said.

"Me, too."

"And I'm sorry for rushing you out of there. I just…" Didn't want to be serious anymore. Didn't want to continue with those weighty subjects. Now he wanted only to enjoy her. He offered her a grin, and then lowered his face to hers. She was centimeters away, so close he could feel the heat of her skin, catch the floral notes of her perfume. And the words he wanted to say went right out of his head. "Oh, Stace, you distract me."

She smiled, that intoxicating smile that was imprinted on his memory. "I'm not trying to."

He reached up and cupped her jaw. His thumbs traced over her bottom lip, and his heart stuttered. "You distract me just by standing there."

The smile widened. "You do the same to me. It's a

wonder I haven't poured a cup of coffee on myself. Or dropped an order on the floor every time you look at me or talk to me."

"There's no coffee here right now. No orders to fill. Nothing but us."

"I noticed." The words escaped her in a breath.

He knew he should pull back. Let her go. Go back to being friends and coworkers, and stop muddying the waters. But as he looked down into her eyes, he couldn't think of a single reason why that was a good idea. He closed the gap between them, let his arms drift down to her back, and pulled Stace Kettering into him until his lips met hers and the world stopped.

CHAPTER TEN

STACE Kettering was falling. Tumbling down, and down, and down, falling hard for Riley McKenna.

When he kissed her, the world came to a stop. She leaned into him, and fire ignited in the spaces where their bodies met. His hands roamed her back, sliding over her hips, her buttocks, and she pressed closer, held tighter.

God help her, but she wanted him. Now. In the worst possible way.

Riley drew back long enough to take a breath and nod toward the guest house. "Maybe Jeremy can wait a few minutes."

"Or a lot of minutes," she said. Who was this brazen woman, who made it clear she wanted a man? Who took his hand and ran headlong for the house like a love struck teenager? Who didn't think about the consequences, but just…desired?

Riley pressed Stace to the door, blindly fumbling to get the key in the lock, while he kept on kissing her. She grasped his shirt, wishing she could tug it off now, but then the door was open and they were tumbling into the house and rushing to get the door shut. In a few quick steps, they were at the sofa, and Riley was drawing her down onto his lap and her dress was hiking up over her thighs, leaving the skin deliciously bare to his touch, and she quit thinking.

His erection was hard against her, and she moaned into his mouth, shifting her position until he moaned, too. His hands tangled in her hair, hers went to his shirt, working the buttons until his skin was exposed to her touch. Breathless, she pulled back, and trailed kisses along his neck, over his shoulders, down his chest. Riley groaned, then hauled her back up, and kissed her so hard, so fast, her head spun.

His warm palms snaked under her dress with slow, easy, sensual moves. Every bit of skin he touched seemed to ignite, and Stace had to remind herself to breathe. Then he cupped her breasts through the lace of her bra, and she gasped. "Riley, oh, God, Riley. Oh—" She had no other words, no coherent thoughts.

"You are beautiful," he murmured against her skin, leaving her mouth long enough to trail kisses down her neck, over the soft jersey of her dress, then to the crest of her breasts. She arched against him, wanting more, wanting his mouth everywhere.

His fingers went to the clasp at her back. Hot anticipation filled her, driving a pounding, insistent need. How long had it been since she'd been touched? Kissed like this?

Then her gaze went to the glass patio doors. Her reflection shimmered back at her. Wanton, uninhibited—

Foolish.

How many times did she have to lose her head, before she got a clue? She scrambled off Riley's lap and pulled her dress down. Her lips were tender from his kisses, and her pulse thundered a protest in her head. "What do you want, Riley?"

He chuckled. "I'd think that was obvious. I want you,

Stace." He reached for her, caught her fingertips, and tugged her toward him.

But she remained resolute and stayed where she was. "I meant from this." She gestured between them. "Is this just one more notch in your belt, or do you want more?"

"I'm not looking to get married tonight." He let out a nervous laugh. "Come on, let's just enjoy what we have."

Hot tears rose in her eyes. She'd been so, so wrong about him. She'd let herself get distracted again by the messages she thought she was reading in a man's eyes. Once again, she'd read an ending that he wasn't even thinking. God, how could she be so stupid? "That's the trouble. We'll enjoy it for the night, but then when the morning comes, what do we have?"

"A really nice memory."

She shook her head, and willed the tears to stay at bay until she could get out of the room. "I want more than a memory," she said. "I want something that stays, that I can depend on. And you, Riley McKenna, are anything but dependable."

Then she ran out of the room, and shut her bedroom door so he wouldn't hear her crying.

Saturday morning dawned.

Unfortunately.

Stace had done her best to avoid Riley after their date. He'd gone to his grandmother's to retrieve Jeremy. She had taken the coward's way out while he was gone—and gone to bed. This morning, she'd headed out the door before Riley was even up, arriving at the diner before Frank. "You're in early," he'd said. "You do know we open later on Saturdays, don't you?"

"I'm too used to getting up early, I guess," Stace said. She avoided Frank's inquisitive gaze and got busy setting up the tables for the morning. As she did, she came across a newspaper tucked between the wall and one of the booths—probably a customer's, stuffed away and forgotten, and missed in the daily cleanup.

Stace tugged it out and turned to toss the week-old issue of the *Herald* into the trash. As she did, her gaze caught on a familiar image.

Riley. With another woman. Her skirt was hiked halfway to her knees, her head was thrown back in laughter, and her hands were on Riley's shoulders—with no mistaking they were together. Nausea rolled in Stace's stomach. She thrust the paper deep into the trash, then turned away.

That could have been her in that picture. Could have been Stace's image under the Playboy Finds A Good Time At Benefit Event headline. She'd come so close last night to falling for him.

For being another of a hundred women in his arms. Just like she had done before.

By the time Riley strolled in, a few minutes before they opened, she had herself firmly in work mode. No longer thinking about where those kisses could have gone last night.

Definitely not thinking about that. Not now, not ever.

A group of women doing a walking tour of the city came in right behind Riley. Stace took the table of eight, glad for the interruption. The morning continued like that, with a steady stream of customers.

A little after eleven, the diner slowed down, and Stace headed to the counter for a quick bite to eat. Frank slid a plate of pancakes over to her. "Heated up the syrup for you."

She smiled. "Thanks." She forked up a thick bite,

chewed, and swallowed. As she did, she noticed a flyer sitting on the counter. "Hey, what's that?"

Frank picked it up. "One of those travel club things. Bunch of old people running around the world."

"Sounds like fun."

Frank waved it off. "Eleanor Givens is always trying to talk me into going to Europe with her."

Stace grinned. Eleanor was in here every Saturday morning, one of the first customers of the day. She usually sat at the counter, and chatted with Frank the whole time. "I think that's because she likes you."

Frank waved the flyer again. "Nah."

"She's looking for a round-the-world travel buddy."

"She should look somewhere else. I don't much like her company." Frank grimaced. "Though I had an interesting conversation with Riley's grandmother the other day. Nice lady. And she likes to travel, too."

"You should invite her to Europe then. I bet she'd say yes."

"And what, leave this place? I'll be here till the day I die." Then his face crumpled. "Aw, Stace, I'm sorry, I didn't mean that."

"It's okay." Her smile wavered, then she brightened, and leaned toward the man she'd known nearly all her life. "You really need to take care of you, Frank, and stop worrying about me."

"I do."

She arched a brow. "So when are you retiring again?"

"Looking to get rid of me?"

"Looking for you to take one of those trips you talk about…and never take."

He shrugged, and got busy refilling a sugar dispenser. It was usually Stace's job, which meant Frank was avoiding the subject. "Traveling the world takes money. I have some savings, but I'm not exactly Rockefeller."

"Why don't you let me buy you out then?"

"We'll talk about that later."

She let out a gust. "You always say that, Frank."

The bell over the door rang, and Walter strode in, letting out his usual greeting of a grunt before heading for his favorite table. Before Stace could head to the booth, Walter waved over Riley.

Frank leaned close and lowered his voice. "Looks like Walter has a new favorite."

"Passing fancy."

Frank quirked a grin at her. "Is that what it is? A passing fancy?"

Stace waved at the corner booth, where Walter was chatting with Riley. Walter was nodding and moving his hands as he talked, animated customer now instead of grumpy older man. Whatever he was talking to Riley about, Walter was passionate about the topic. "You know Walter, he's always finding something new to complain about. He—"

"I didn't mean Walter. I meant you and Riley."

Stace toyed with her order pad. "There's nothing between me and Riley."

Frank let out a guffaw. "Yeah, right. I may be old, but I'm not blind, and there is something brewing between you two. Why, it's like the Morning Glory's own little soap opera."

"You are definitely imagining things." She slid off the stool and tucked her order pad back into the pocket of her apron. "I better go over there and make sure he's not riling Walter up."

Frank snorted. "Yep. That's exactly why you're going over there."

Stace ignored Frank. He had a tendency to play matchmaker with every man who expressed an interest in Stace. That was all that was. Frank's wishful thinking that she'd get married, settle down, and have a few kids he could spoil mercilessly.

She headed for the coffee station. The carafes were nearly empty, so she put on a new pot of both regular and decaf. She sensed Riley behind her before she heard him.

"Looked like a pretty serious conversation there with Frank," he said.

"It's nothing. Just the same-old, same-old, of me bugging him to retire." She tossed the used coffee grounds into the trash, then cleaned the area around the coffee station. "Once I get enough money saved, I want to buy out his half. Then he won't have any excuse not to travel the world." She sighed. "I just need business to pick up enough to afford that."

"Well, I think I can help with that. Remember the idea I was looking for? I thought—"

"I'm not getting any younger here. Can I get my coffee?" Walter called to Riley. *"Please?"*

Riley laughed. "Guess I'm rubbing off on Walter."

"You have a tendency to do that with people."

"What about you? Do I rub off on you?"

"You…made an impression."

He arched a brow. "A good one?"

"Keep Walter waiting too long and he won't leave you a tip." She had finished loading the coffee station, and turned away to rinse out the empty pots.

"Walter can wait for me to get your answer."

"He'll be waiting an awful long time then." She didn't want to talk to Riley. She wanted to avoid him and the images that picture had risen in her head, until Riley moved on to the next thing, the next woman. Surely she could keep from falling for the man, or at least, falling any more than she already had.

The man had all the permanence of chalk on the sidewalk. One good storm, and he'd disappear.

"You know," Riley said, unaware of Stace's thoughts—or her fervent wish that he would just go away—as he leaned against the counter while he waited on Walter's coffee to brew, "it's taken me a few days, but I finally realize why Walter looks so familiar to me."

"Oh, really?" Stupid coffeepot, which was probably older than Frank, had blinked off and refused to turn on. She fiddled with the switch, then reached behind and unplugged it, and replugged it into the wall. Still no response.

"It took me a while to put it together, but—" Riley gave the side of the coffee station a hard tap, and the machine leapt to life "—once I did, it gave me an idea."

"Hey, I don't have all day to wait for my coffee, you know." Walter's crabby voice carried through the diner again.

"One second, Walter. New coffee is brewing just for you." Riley shot Stace a grin. "What if I told you I had a way to turn Walter into the nicest customer you ever had? And also serve your goal of getting more business into this place. I'll need your help to pull it off, though."

"I don't know."

He paused to look at her as he poured the dark brew into a mug. "Just trust me. Please."

Trust him. That was where she got into trouble, every time. She'd trusted him on moving in to his guest house, and look where that had led. She'd trusted him on letting him work with her, and now she was forced to see him every day—until he gave up on this job and moved on to the next. She'd trusted him when he'd kissed her, and very nearly believed those kisses were real.

"Please," he whispered in her ear.

How she wanted to resist that deep baritone. But her heart quickened and her pulse leapt and a smile winged its way across her face, without her permission. "Okay."

As soon as they reached Walter's table, Riley plopped down the hot cup before him. "Good morning, Walter."

Walter snorted. "Don't try to cheer me up."

"Why not? It's a gorgeous day, and you're alive. Enough reason to celebrate, isn't it?"

He snorted again.

Riley leaned against the high back of the opposite seat. "You know, Walter, you'd think a guy who works with animals all day would be more...cheery."

Walter arched a brow, clearly surprised that Riley knew his occupation. Beside Riley, Stace held her own surprise in check. How had Riley learned that information? In all the time she'd served Walter, the only personal detail he'd shared was his addiction to kosher dill pickles.

"To me, animals are nicer than people," Walter said.

"That may very well be true," Riley said, then he slid into the booth opposite Walter, making enough room for Stace to join him. "But Stace and I have been thinking that it might be good to combine the two."

Walter sipped the hot coffee. "What do you mean?"

"You have a fundraiser coming up."

Now he had Walter's interest. The older man leaned back and propped an elbow on the banquette. "How do you know that?"

"My brother Finn has one of your dogs, a Golden named Heidi. Sweetest dog you've ever seen. She's a frequent guest at my grandmother's house, and Finn talks up the shelter every chance he gets."

"I agree," Stace said. "She's a lovely dog."

"Finn, as in Finn McKenna? He's one of our biggest supporters." Walter regarded Riley with new eyes. "You're his brother?"

"Yep."

Walter leaned forward. "And how exactly does that matter to me?"

"You need a place for your fundraiser. Finn mentioned that the shelter doesn't really have a good place to hold a big event, and your usual venue shut down unexpectedly last week. That leaves you high and dry, and probably scrambling for a location."

"We were planning on canceling." Walter scowled. "And yes, that has made me a little grumpy."

Riley smiled. "I wouldn't cancel just yet, not until you consider my idea."

Walter crossed his hands on the table. "I'm listening."

Stace glanced at Riley. What was he up to? "Me, too."

"You need something that will draw folks in, and you also need volunteers. I was thinking—" at this, Riley glanced at Stace "—maybe the Morning Glory would be a great place to hold it. The diner would get some publicity, there'd be food to lure people in, the shelter would get the bonus of a highly trafficked location, and on top of that, I think I could round up some extra volunteers to help with the dogs."

Walter scowled. "You can't have dogs in this place."

"You can on the outdoor patio," Stace said, leapfrogging onto Riley's train of thought. Why had she never thought to have events like this on the weekends? Using the Morning Glory for more than just a breakfast and lunch place could really boost sales and exposure. "The patio never gets used because we're a little understaffed right now. It's out back, but has street access."

"And if you held it on Tuesday afternoon, like you originally planned," Riley added, "you'd have all that traffic from the workers heading home."

When he paused, Stace leapt in again. "The diner is usually closed after lunch service, so if we're open for this event, we could bring in some business we normally don't have."

Walter mulled the idea. "You said you had volunteers."

"Stace knows someone who would love to design some posters for you, and I suspect, help with the animals, too." Riley's blue gaze held hers. "He's a bright kid, with a lot of artistic ability, and even better, he's got a lot of friends who would be good helpers."

Tears threatened the back of her eyes at Riley's thoughtfulness in including her nephew, a boy who was seeking approval, acceptance, purpose. It would be the perfect thing for Jeremy to be involved in. Something that would give him a positive outlet for his art. "Oh, yes. Definitely."

Walter drummed his fingers on the table. "Let me talk to my board, get back to you tomorrow."

"Sounds good." Riley and Stace slid out of the seat.

"In the meantime, I want some more coffee. Hot as you can make it. And don't make me wait all damned day this time." Walter went back to his paper, clearly done with today's human interaction.

Stace pulled Riley aside by the coffeepot. "How on earth did you come up with that idea?"

"I overheard Walter talking on his cell phone the other day. He was complaining about how he didn't have enough help for the fundraiser and the venue had let him down. Once I realized what fundraiser it was, I thought maybe there'd be a way to help. Then I thought the best way to help one is to help—" he grinned "—two."

"The shelter and the diner."

He nodded. "Hopefully it's a win-win all around."

"It's a brilliant idea." Riley's idea was exactly what both the shelter and the Morning Glory needed. "Thank you."

Riley's blue eyes met hers, and for a second she forgot that she wanted to stay away from him. Forgot that he might be good for the diner, but he was bad for her heart. "You know, for this to work, I'm going to need your help."

"My help? What am I going to do?"

"Convince Jeremy to do the posters, and help me with the marketing materials."

"I don't know anything about marketing materials." Stace handed Riley a clean mug, and he filled it with steaming hot coffee. "That's supposed to be your area."

"You know about this diner," he said. "Convince me why the Morning Glory is the best place on earth, or at least in the city of Boston, to eat. After that, we'll convince the world." He put up a hand. "You don't have to tell me now. Wait till lunch. We'll talk then. Okay?"

"Okay."

"Good. Then it's a date." Before she could respond, he was gone, headed to Walter's table with a fresh cup of coffee. She didn't want to have lunch with Riley. Or work on a project with him. She was trying to stay away from him, so her foolish body wouldn't betray her every time he was near. She glanced at the trash, and even though she could no longer see the image on the newspaper, she knew it was there. A reminder to redouble her resolve.

But as the morning and early afternoon passed, and Stace bustled around the diner, she found herself getting excited about the idea of the fundraiser. If the Morning Glory could turn the corner on profits, it might be enough to allow her to buy Frank out. Then she could finally take care of the man who had taken care of her for so many years.

It would, of course, mean putting her own life on hold again for a while, but at this rate, she was getting used to that. She'd done it for her sister, now for Jeremy, and soon, for Frank. She glanced around the diner that had been her father's dream, and heart. Maybe someday down the road there'd be time for Stace to fall in love, get married, have a family. Just not today.

Riley was across the room, talking to an elderly woman. He smiled, and the woman smiled in response. Infectious, that's what Riley was, and for a second, she envied the woman who had his attention. Then Stace shrugged off the emotion. He didn't want the same life she did, and wishing for a different ending would only leave her disappointed in the end.

Her cell phone buzzed in her pocket. Her tables didn't need anything for the moment, so Stace ducked out of the diner to take the call. The number was unfamiliar, and for a second, Stace's heart plummeted, sure that something had happened to Jeremy. "Hello?"

"Stace?" Lisa's voice. Wavering, unsure. So welcome after weeks of silence.

Still, Stace braced herself. If her sister was calling, it could only mean one thing—she needed money or a place to crash. How many times had they danced this dance? She loved her sister, but she couldn't be a refuge for Lisa, not anymore. It did nothing but give Lisa per-mission to keep on hurting herself, and that was something Stace could no longer watch. "Lisa, if you need money or a place to stay, I can't help you. You have to help yourself first."

"I'm doing that, Stace, really." The connection crackled and her voice echoed, sounding more like a payphone than a cell phone or regular landline. Had Lisa lost her cell again? Was she in some seedy neighborhood, waiting for rescue?

Again, Stace resisted the urge to help. "Good. I'm glad." She tried to work some enthusiasm into her voice. She had heard the same words a thousand times. Would this time stick? Or would Lisa break Jeremy's heart again?

"How's Jeremy?" Lisa asked.

"He's doing good. He got a scholarship to the Wilmont Academy and he's loving it there."

"He did?" Lisa's voice broke, with pride, with regret, Stace wasn't sure. "That's perfect for him. He's always loved to draw. I used to think he'd grow up to be an artist. Oh, he must be so happy."

"He's getting there," Stace said. He'd be happier if his mom was there and clean, but Stace didn't add that.

"I want to see him," Lisa said. "I miss him so much."

Now the anger did rise in Stace. She thought of all the times she had bailed out her sister. Given her money, food, a place to stay. Helped her raise her son. And then picked up the pieces when Lisa had left Jeremy behind. "You can't just do this, Lisa. You can't walk out of his life one day and walk back in the next. He's a kid. He needs stability. A mother he can depend on. And you haven't been any of those things."

"I love him."

Stace pressed a hand to her forehead. Damn, the words hurt, but they needed to be said. "Loving him means being a good mother. Instead of someone selfish enough to put drugs in front of their family. Get cleaned up, and maybe we can talk." The anger became a tide, built up over the past month, in every moment that Stace had had to comfort her nephew or fill in as surrogate mom. It should have been Lisa who'd dropped him off that day at the new school. Should have been Lisa making Jeremy pancakes and making sure he took his vitamins. "You dumped your own son in my lap after the car accident—"

"I'm sorry, Stace. That accident really shook me up and—"

"And you haven't spoken to any of us in a month." Stace sighed. She couldn't listen to the excuses, the pleas, anymore. "I love you but I can't do this anymore, Lisa. I really can't."

"Stace, I *am* better. You don't understand—"

But Stace had heard enough. Year after year, the same story, the same excuses. "Bye, Lisa." Then she hung up the phone and put it in her pocket. Her heart broke, and she wanted so badly to call Lisa back, to apologize, to smooth the waters like she had every time before. But then she thought of her nephew, of the heartbreak in his face the day his mother left, and knew she couldn't put Jeremy or herself through that anymore.

Riley poked his head out the diner door. "Hey, you okay?"

"Yeah. Just dealing with some…family stuff."

"Want to talk about it?"

She looked at Riley's tall frame, his broad shoulders, his hard chest, his soft blue eyes, and a part of her wanted so badly to curl into him and tell him everything. To let someone else share the burden for a while. "I'm okay."

He came outside, and waited for the door to shut before speaking. "You don't look okay."

"I handled it." Had she? All she'd done was hang up on her sister. She hadn't changed anything, not really.

He moved until his shadow draped over them both, like a cool blanket. "Why don't we talk for a little while?" He gestured toward the bench that sat outside the diner.

"We should get back to work."

"It's not a crime to rely on somebody else for a little while. You don't have to carry every burden by yourself, Stace."

"I'll be fine by myself," she said. "I always am."

Then she went back inside before she could give in to the temptation of Riley McKenna. Stace poured herself into work, which helped some to take her mind off of her sister. But not off of Riley.

She watched him from the corner of her eye, always, always aware of him just across the crowded room.

An hour later, the diner was deserted. Riley pulled two plates of burgers off the dividing wall between the kitchen and the diner, and brought them over to the booth where Stace had sat down. "Lunch is served."

She gave him a grateful smile. "Should I count the fries?"

"I already stole one of yours on the way over here. You can take it out of my pay."

She laughed, then heaped a generous portion of ketchup on the corner of her plate and began dipping and eating her fries. They melted like heaven in her mouth. The burger was amazing, as usual. "If I eat too many of these, you'll have to roll me home."

He laughed. "Maybe we'll become human bowling balls, and race down the street."

"Now, there's an advertisement for the food here." To punctuate the point, she downed another fry.

Riley leaned back in his seat and stretched. "If we're going to have that race, we'll have to do it before Wednesday."

"Why?" She swirled the last fry in the ketchup puddle.

"I put in my notice with Frank this morning. Turns out there's a big project over at McKenna Media, and they called me in to help with it."

"You got your old job back?" Disbelief tinged her words. He wasn't staying.

"I proved my grandmother's point. I got a job on my own, earned some income." Then he leaned forward and met her gaze. "You knew this was a temporary position for me. Frank's okay with it. He wished me well and everything. So what's wrong?"

"Are you happy there?"

He scoffed. "Who's happy in their job?"

"I am. It's hard work, yes, and it doesn't always pay well, but at the end of the day, I look around this place and think of all the people who have left here full, content, and happy, and that makes me feel full, contented, and happy. It started out as my father's dream, and somewhere along the way it became mine." Stace wrapped her hands around her glass of ice water. "Anyway, that's what I hope people feel when they're here."

"I think they do," he said. "Everybody but Walter anyway."

She laughed, then cursed Riley for making her laugh while he was also breaking her heart. "True."

Riley pushed his empty plate to the side, then pulled out a small notepad and pen. "Okay, now on to the reason for our lunch. To spread the word of the Morning

Glory's awesomeness to the city of Boston." He clicked the pen. "What do you think makes the Morning Glory special?"

"The burgers. The atmosphere. The service." She gave Riley a smile, but it was a weaker one than before. He was leaving, she needed to remember that.

"I meant to you, personally. Why is your heart in this place? Because it reminds you of your dad?"

In every corner, she could see a memory. Her father plopping her onto one of the counter stools, and spinning her in a circle. Sitting in a corner booth, doing her homework after school. Pushing a mop around that was bigger than her, just to help her dad at the end of the day. "Do you know where the name Morning Glory comes from?"

Riley shook his head.

"My dad used to call me Morning Glory. Whenever I woke up, he'd say, 'Good morning, glory,' as if the sun had just risen in front of him. My mother loved flowers, and I guess that's where it came from. He said I reminded him of the best parts of starting his day. So when he and Frank opened this place, they wanted that same atmosphere here." She glanced around the room, at the painted violet morning glories that ran along the ceiling, the bright blue seat cushions that had been there since the day they opened, and the pale yellow countertops that had served thousands of meals. "It's just a really special place to me."

"It's your life," Riley said.

She let out a long breath. "Yes, I suppose it is. There are days when the only thing I think about is this place and how to make it succeed."

"You know, if you changed a few things, that might help. Add free Wi-Fi, for instance, for all the businesspeople. Change out the paint color, switch up the menu to offer some healthier foods." He offered her a grin. "I may not have been the most useful employee at McKenna Media, but I did pick up some marketing ideas. Change isn't always a bad thing, you know." He squared up his silverware. "Maybe then the Morning Glory wouldn't consume your life. What do you think that has cost you?"

The conversation had taken a sudden detour, going down a road Stace never visited. After her sister's phone call earlier, the arrow hit especially deep. How much had all this cost her?

Too much.

But she'd be damned if she was going to tell Riley that. He was leaving and when he was gone, she had no doubt she'd be another distant memory in a mental crowd of blondes, brunettes, and redheads.

"It takes a lot to keep this place running," she said, instead of the truth, "but—"

"That's not what I meant. You've poured your whole self into this diner. And I bet that's come at a huge personal sacrifice."

"This doesn't help with marketing materials."

"No, but it helps me understand you."

She got to her feet. "You don't need to understand me. You just need to—" She cut off the words and turned away.

Riley grabbed her wrist and stopped her. "I need to do what?"

"Just do what you do best, Riley. And quit." Then she walked away before she let him see how much saying that had cost her.

CHAPTER ELEVEN

THE day of the rescue shelter's fundraiser dawned bright and sunny. Jeremy had moaned and groaned about helping, but in the end, he'd made three times the number of posters they needed, and was ready before Stace.

Riley had followed her request and stayed away. Stace had spent her free time swimming, logging lap after lap until exhaustion claimed her and she collapsed into bed at the end of the day. Riley spent the hours after work with Jeremy, creating posters and working on some "secret" project in the garage of Riley's grandmother's house. Whatever it was, the two of them had kept it from Stace. Her nephew had never been so excited about a project before, and for that, Stace was grateful to Riley. He'd lit a fire in her nephew. She could see the positive effects of that change in the way Jeremy held his head up, the way he talked, and most of all, the way he smiled.

But once Jeremy was in bed, Riley had headed out on the town. Stace would lie in her room, trying not to cry when she heard the front door shut and Riley's car start. She was sure she'd done the right thing in ending their relationship. Then why did it hurt so much?

"You're slow and Riley's not even out here yet,"

Jeremy said that morning when Stace entered the kitchen. "There are people waiting on us, you know."

Stace put a palm to her nephew's head. "Are you sick?"

"No." He laughed. "Not at all, Aunt Stace."

"Then why are you suddenly so responsible?" She perched a fist on her hip and eyed him. "Did my nephew get replaced by his alien pod twin?"

"I just..." Jeremy shrugged. "I really want this to go well. You know, 'cause it's for, like, abandoned animals."

Stace's heart constricted. She drew Jeremy into a hug. "I understand. I totally do."

Jeremy wrangled his way out of the embrace, but Stace could see a smile on his lips. As he headed out the door, he passed by their packed bags. The roofer was scheduled to finish up today. Once the fundraiser was over, she'd come back here, grab their bags, and return to the little house in Dorchester. She should have been relieved, but a part of her was sad.

Was it because she'd gotten used to living in this cozy little house? Or gotten used to being around Riley? That alone was a sign she needed to get back to her normal life—Riley would do nothing but break her heart in the end. He was leaving the diner tomorrow, replaced by Irene, who had found a babysitter and was anxious to get back to work. Riley would be gone, and before she knew it, hopefully he'd become a distant memory.

He'd made it clear, over and over, that he wasn't a guy who committed, and if there was one thing Stace had been all her life, it was committed. To the diner. To that house. To her family.

Hadn't he gone out again last night? It was probably why he was dragging a little this morning. Instead of waiting in the house to find out the answer, Stace waited outside for Riley, then the three of them headed over to the diner, taking Riley's car instead of the train, since traffic into the city was light in the mid-afternoon, and because Riley told her he had the "special project" in the back.

"Today should be busy," Riley said. "There was a write-up in the paper yesterday about it, and my brother said Walter's been talking it up to anyone who will listen."

"I bet you were hoping to end your last day on a less hectic note," she said.

"I don't mind working. Especially for a good cause." Riley rested his hands on the steering wheel. "This event has energized me. I'm excited about it."

"So excited you had to go out and celebrate last night. And the night before. And the night before that." She could have bit her tongue for saying what she did, for letting him know that she cared how he spent his time.

"It wasn't about that," Riley said. "When I went out, it was to—"

"I don't need an explanation. Let's just get through the day." She turned and kept her gaze on the road passing by her window. And the conversation ended.

By the time they arrived, Frank had already started cooking and Walter had his team in the back, setting up portable pens. Several volunteers wearing T-shirts emblazoned with the shelter's logo were unloading animals and setting up an adoption station.

A half dozen of Jeremy's new school friends had come by to help. Within moments, the nonchalant teenagers smiled and laughed as they interacted with the dogs and cats. Stace grinned at the sight of a burly football-player-type holding a shivering schnauzer, and talking softly to calm the little dog's jitters.

Stace and Riley headed into the Morning Glory, and returned with platters of fresh baked muffins and donuts, laying them out on tables beside steaming pots of coffee. They had priced them reasonably, and agreed to donate the profits to the rescue organization. Every person who took a treat got a small flyer advertising the Morning Glory's regular specials, and featuring Frank's award-winning burgers front and center.

As more and more people stopped by for the goodies and asked about the Morning Glory's menu, Stace had to admit that Riley had surprised her. He'd put together a successful event, in very little time, and she felt bad for giving him a hard time about going out. He had clearly spent a lot of his free time on planning the event and marketing it. When there was a lull in the activity, she slid over to where he was refilling the carafes. "You did great with this."

He shrugged. "I didn't do much. The shelter had a lot of the groundwork done already."

"The radio station is here, the TV station, too. And I think I see reporters from all the major papers. More pets have left here with new owners than I can count. Plus, you've got people buzzing about the Morning Glory in ways they never have before."

"That was the goal."

"It worked. And I'm sorry for giving you a hard time this morning."

"That's okay. Apology accepted."

"Good." She'd accomplished her purpose. She'd thanked him and she'd apologized. She should leave, and put some distance between herself and Riley before she was tempted into ignoring the warning bells in her head. Still, she lingered. "So, uh, where's this special project I've heard so much about?"

Riley glanced at Jeremy. The foot traffic had slowed, and only a couple of people milled around the adoption area. "Hey, Jeremy, do you think it's time?"

Jeremy grinned. "Yeah." The two walked around the other side of the building, while Stace waited by the table and nursed a cup of coffee. A few minutes later, they came back, each carrying the end of something long and covered by an old sheet.

Frank came up behind Stace. "What the hell is that?"

"A special project." She shrugged. "I don't know what, exactly. They kept the whole thing a secret from me."

Riley and Jeremy paused by Stace, tipped the item in their hands to one side, and stood it on its end. Then Riley stepped back and gestured to Jeremy. "You do the honors. You did the work."

Jeremy nodded, then tugged the sheet, revealing a tall, thin wooden curio stand, with turned spindles and a carved top. Sunlight bounced off the gleaming wood and its newly shellacked finish.

Stace stepped forward, running her finger over the shape forming the top. "Is that...?"

Jeremy raised one shoulder, let it drop. "It's supposed to be a bunch of morning glories."

She traced the outline of the trio of circular flowers and their blossoming bright centers. She could feel the ridges of the hand-working, the careful detail put into each one. "Oh, my goodness, they're beautiful."

"Pretty damned amazing, I think, kiddo," Frank said.

"It's supposed to be a shelf for you to put all those cups on," Jeremy said. "You know the ones you have in the house on your dresser?"

"My mother's teacups. Oh, Jeremy, that's so sweet." She pressed a hand to her mouth, while tears rushed to the back of her eyes. She lifted her gaze to Riley. "Thank you."

"Don't thank me. I made him do all the work." He thumbed toward Jeremy.

A measure of pride shone in Jeremy's eyes, then he dropped his gaze and toed at the ground. "Riley helped me. A lot."

"It's beautiful," she said again, and touched first one shelf, then the other. Already she could see the teacups seated there, proudly displayed as they always should have been. "I didn't know you knew how to do that."

"I didn't," Jeremy said. "But Riley did. He said it'd be a good thing for me to learn, because I like art and stuff, and this was art, but with wood." Jeremy ran a hand over the carved flowers. "It kinda is, isn't it?"

"It's a masterpiece is what it is," Frank said, clapping Jeremy on the back. "You did a good job, son."

"I agree. It *is* a masterpiece." Stace gave her nephew a big hug. For the first time, he didn't wriggle out of the embrace, and Stace marveled again at the positive changes Riley had brought into Jeremy's life. "I'm going to put this front and center in the house as soon as we get home tonight."

Home. Back to the little house in Dorchester. The thought saddened her—not because she didn't love that little house with all its flaws, the same house where she'd grown up, but because it would mean closing a chapter on her life. Maybe it was time to sell that house, to move on to something new. She glanced at her nephew, and decided it was time for all of them to try something new. "I think you did an incredible job, Jeremy."

"Thanks." Jeremy shifted from foot to foot, clearly uncomfortable with the praise. Then his eyes widened and he let out a gasp. "Mom?"

Stace's heart caught in her throat, and she hesitated a moment to pray, to hope, before she turned.

Lisa.

Her little sister stood on the sidelines, looking unsure, almost scared. And better than she had in five years. She had put on some weight and her hair was no longer a dyed carrot-red, but back to her natural blond color. Stace hesitated only a second, then closed the gap between them and put out her arms. "Hey, sis."

Lisa broke into tears, then dove into Stace's hug with a fierce, tight embrace. "Oh, God, I've missed you so much. You and Jeremy."

"Where have you been? You look terrific." She really did. Her face had lost that gaunt, drawn pallor. She looked alive, vibrant. Hope bloomed in Stace's chest. "You really look amazing, Lisa."

"Thanks." A watery smile filled Lisa's face. "I'm sorry I left without telling you where I went. I was so afraid that if I said anything, I'd jinx it, or I'd chicken out." She let out a long breath, and her smile wavered. "I went to rehab. Spent thirty days in, and now I'm enrolled in an outpatient program at a halfway house. I'm doing it this time, Stace. I really am." Lisa held up a chip that celebrated her thirty days of sobriety, clenching it as if it was a lifeline. Then she turned to her son, who stood a little to the side, not yet sure about his mother's return. "I can't miss one more day of your life, Jeremy, and I swear I won't. The day I left was a huge wake-up call for me. I almost killed my son that day because I was stupid and selfish and messed-up." Her voice caught on a sob, then she put a hand on Jeremy's shoulder, and the rest of her words poured out in a teary, heartfelt rush. "I don't ever want to be that mother again. I love you, Jeremy. I really do."

Then Jeremy stepped forward, moving slowly at first, then faster, until his arms were around his mother and she was crying onto his shoulder. His face reddened and tears brimmed in his eyes but the big, wide, growing smile on his face kept the tears at bay. Soon, all three of them were crying and hugging, with Lisa telling them in halting, excited sentences about the lessons she had learned and the changes she was going to make. For the first time in forever, Stace believed the change was real, lasting. Lisa had a long road ahead of her, but Stace had a feeling this time she was going to make it.

As Stace watched their reunion, a sad lump sank in her stomach. Jeremy was gone, Lisa was okay, and Stace was left...

Exactly where she'd been before. With her life on hold. How long would she keep on doing that?

Stace left Jeremy and Lisa to catch up, and returned to Riley and Frank. They were serving the last of the food to the shelter volunteers, who had begun loading up the remaining animals and cleaning up from the day. "Jeremy's mom?" Riley asked.

Stace nodded. "I guess it's true what they say."

"What's that?"

"Miracles can come true."

Riley's gaze met hers and held. "I think you're right. They can."

What did he mean by that? She wanted to ask, but didn't. He was leaving, after all, and the sooner she learned to let go, the better.

Frank cleared his throat. "Seems we're low on muffins. I better get back inside and get some more food for the troops." Frank headed into the Morning Glory, leaving Riley and Stace alone. Clearly, on purpose.

When Frank was gone, Stace turned back to the shelf.

"Was this your idea?" she asked, running a hand down the smooth surface of the shelf. It was as if Riley had read her mind. He'd created something that would hold her most precious mementos, one that featured her father's morning glories.

Why did he keep doing things that worked their way into her heart, even as she tried to forget him? "What made you build this, of all things?"

"You needed someplace strong and secure to put those teacups. Something better than a flimsy shelf in the bedroom."

"Well, now that I'll have a better roof, they should be safe." But was she safe? Had she fallen too far to be able to forget Riley after he left?

"Good. That's what I wanted." He placed a hand on the carving at the top. "I'm glad Jeremy enjoyed making it."

"He did. I think you inspired a new hobby in him." She cocked her head and studied Riley. "Who taught you?"

Riley pinched the flower at the center of the shelf, as if he could pluck it from its wooden home. But it didn't move, of course, and he finally released the faux flower. "My dad. That was our thing. We worked on all kinds of projects. Just before he died, we started building a tree house."

"That must have been fun."

"It was." His voice dropped into a quieter range as the memories flooded back. As he talked, Stace and he walked together to the corner of the building, far from the remaining people. "There was this woodpecker that would come and tap at the tree above our heads while we were working. Darn thing was there every single day. My dad called it the house mascot. He even built a little birdhouse and attached it to the tree house, so the woodpecker could stay." A soft smile stole over Riley's face at the memory. "Then my dad died. I went back to the tree house after the funeral, but the woodpecker wasn't there. I went back every single day, and tried to finish the tree house myself, thinking if I did, the woodpecker would come back. But he never did." Riley let out a low curse, then shook his head. "I stopped building things that day. Stopped…"

"Stopped what?"

"Stopped counting on things to be the same." He lifted his gaze to her and in his eyes, she saw the glimmer of unshed tears. "Nothing lasts, Stace, that's what I learned that day. *Nothing* lasts."

It all made sense in that moment. She saw in Riley the same fears that had plagued her. Who could have known that this man, from the other side of the city, the other side of the social coin, could be so similar to her?

"Oh, Riley." She led him over to the stoop at the back of the diner, and they sat on the cold concrete stub. "Do you know why I still live in that crappy house in Dorchester?"

"Because it's expensive as hell to buy a house in Boston?"

She laughed. "Well, there is that. But no, it's more…" She picked up a stick on the ground and peeled at the bark, stripping the thin piece of wood bare. "It's that I was afraid of the same thing as you. Nothing lasts, I told myself, but I thought that if I held on tight enough to what I had it would. I couldn't let go. I wanted things to stay the same, but I've realized the more I hold on to the same things and the same places, the more it keeps me stuck. Then the roof caved in—literally." She shook her head. "I have done the same thing every single day for eight years, Riley. I have gone to work at the Morning Glory, and gone home. Just like I did for all the years before that. And now today I finally realized why." She lifted her gaze to his, and this time, the tears pushed their way through, fat droplets puddling on her lap. "I was afraid to change. Afraid to take a risk. Afraid to be more, do more."

"Why?"

"Because then I could lose it all. And the only way I could keep my grip on everything I had left was to keep it all exactly the same. So I kept my dad's furniture and my mother's teacups and the same menu, and everything that had been as it was years ago. And guess what?"

He waited, letting her talk, letting her get it out.

"All it did was keep me glued in place. I didn't go to college, I didn't get married, I didn't have kids. I kept telling myself it was because I didn't have time, and maybe, yes, I didn't, but it was really because I was afraid of changing anything." She shook her head. "You were right about me. I let this place become my life. Then I saw my nephew, a boy who has just as much reason as me to try to control his world, embrace a change in school, in his hobbies, in his life, and I realized that change was good. This event, for instance, was the kind of thing I resisted for years because I thought it would destroy the spirit of the Morning Glory, but instead, it made it better. Stronger. It made the Morning Glory something more than it was before. And that's rewarding. It's not just a diner now, it's a part of the community. Because we changed." She met his blue gaze. "Because of you."

"All I had was the idea." He shrugged off the praise.

"Why do you do that? You were a major part of all of this, and you don't take any credit."

"Stace, I didn't do much."

"You did." Then she looked at him, really looked at him, and saw a mirror of herself. "And you know what? I think you're afraid, too."

"Me? No, not at all."

"You are. And that's why you keep running. From jobs. From responsibilities. From labels. From…me."

He looked away. "I'm not afraid of anything."

"Prove it. Take the biggest risk of your life, Riley." She got to her feet and tossed the stick onto the ground. It tumbled end over end into the shadows. "And stick to something. Really stick to it. Forever."

The shelter's fundraiser had been a success, on all fronts. Walter's face curved in something resembling a smile, and Frank strutted around the diner, beaming from ear to ear. "We should do more things like that," Frank said. "It shakes things up around here, and gets people talking."

Stace wrapped up the last of the muffins. Riley was outside, finishing the cleanup. She probably should have been helping him, but truly, she only wanted the day to be over. It was the last day Riley would be working here, and the last day she'd have to deal with the conflicting emotions that being around him awakened.

Riley hadn't followed after she'd issued the challenge. That told her everything she needed to know. Even as her heart shattered and tears threatened her eyes.

"I think it's time we did some things that got people talking," Stace said. Focus on work, on the diner, on things she could depend upon. "Maybe change up the menu. Give this place a new coat of paint."

Frank leaned back and crossed his arms over his chest. "Wow. Never thought I'd hear you say those words."

"I'm sorry, Frank." She put a hand on his arm. He had been a part of the Morning Glory since day one, and loved it as much as she did. How could she presume dramatic changes were okay? "Maybe we shouldn't change anything. Keep it just the way it's always been."

"Don't you dare," Frank said.

She arched a brow. "What?"

"I *want* you to change things. For this place, for you." He untied his apron and tossed it into the laundry bag. "And for me."

She dropped onto a counter stool, and sat the bag of muffins on her lap. "I've been trying to talk you into change for years." Doing it for someone else had clearly been easier than doing it for herself. But those days were over now. Change was in the air in Stace's life, too.

"I know you have." Frank said. "And I've just been waiting, Stace girl."

"For what?"

"For you to be okay." Frank's face softened, and he lowered himself onto the stool beside her. "It took some time, but now I think you're going to be just fine."

"I've always been fine."

"Nope. You've been pretending, and that ain't the same thing." His hand covered hers, so much bigger and warmer, and always, always there for her. "You've been spending the past eight years taking care of everyone but you. Telling me, and anyone who could listen, that you were fine, you didn't need any help. Then your roof got a big old hole in it, and you had to ask for help."

She let out a little laugh. "I guess literally, huh?"

"Yep." Frank gave her a grin. "Riley turned out to be good for you."

She scoffed. "He turned out to be exactly what I expected. Unreliable. He quit, remember?"

"Yep. And I'm fine with it. He's searching for his purpose. I don't know if he's found it yet, but he's a hundred steps closer than he was the day I hired him."

She shook her head. He didn't know the truth about Riley. "You always see the best in people, Frank."

"Maybe I just see the truth."

She considered that. "Maybe."

Frank reached into his back pocket, pulled out a piece of paper, and plopped it onto the counter between them. "You might want to take out a Help Wanted ad."

Stace picked up the paper, unfolded it, then raised her gaze to Frank's. "You're going? To Europe?"

"Yep. Eleanor talked me into it. Said she'd show me the sights." Frank arched a brow. "Though I think she's got her sights set on me."

Stace laughed. "What made you change your mind? I thought you wanted to wait."

"I *was* waiting. For you."

"Me?"

"For you to be ready for me to leave."

She laughed. "Frank, I'm a grown-up. I'll be fine. I'll miss you like crazy, but I'll be fine."

"I know that. I also know you've been wanting to buy me out for years now."

She put the brochure down. Its bright colors and bold headlines promised the trip of a lifetime, something Frank Simpson deserved. "I'm sorry, but I just don't have enough money yet. I've been saving like crazy, but—"

"Quit that." He grabbed her hand again. "You don't need to buy me out."

"Frank, how are you going to afford retirement? You need—"

"I don't need your money, Stace. Nor do I want it. I don't want you to buy me out. I want to keep on owning a little piece of the Morning Glory. I've been saving, too, you know. And waiting for you to ask me for help."

She shook her head. "Frank, you've done so much, I couldn't ask you for anything else."

"I'm your friend, Stace. Stop taking care of others all the time, and ask someone to take care of you once in a while. And guess what? If you ask me…" His light blue gaze and friendly smile met hers. "I'll be there."

She slid off the stool and wrapped him in a hug. "Oh, Frank, how can I ever repay you?"

"You can make this diner your own. It's not your dad's and mine anymore, it's *yours*. Change the colors, change the menu, change the name, I don't care. Make it your own, and then make it sing, like you always do."

Excitement bubbled inside her. She had no idea what she wanted to do with the Morning Glory, but just the thought of possibilities stirred her mental pot. She turned around, and saw changes in her mind. All these years, she'd resisted moving so much as a chair, but this new Stace, the one who had seen how a few changes could transform a life, a person, a neighborhood, she wanted to keep that momentum going, and let it snowball into a future she couldn't yet see.

"So you're really ready to travel the world?" she asked Frank.

"Yep." He tucked the brochure back into his pocket. "You know I never had kids of my own, but to me, you were always like a daughter."

"Aw, Frank." She hugged the burly chef a second time. "And you're like my second dad."

He drew her tight to him, and held her for a long time. Stace wasn't sure, but she thought she felt a teardrop onto her shoulder. Then Frank drew back, and swiped at his face. His teasing grin was back on his face before anyone could mistake him for getting emotional. "Well, it's time for me to go."

She held on one more time. Change was good, even if it sometimes hurt. She'd miss Frank. A lot. "I know."

"There was one more thing I was waiting for."

"What's that? A compliment from Walter?"

Frank chuckled. "That'd be way too much waiting for me." He paused and the teasing left his features. "No, I was waiting to be sure that you would have your own happy ending."

"I will. I'll be working on the diner and—"

"I meant with love. I wanted to wait to retire, until I knew you had met Mr. Right."

"I didn't—"

He put a finger under her chin, cutting off her protests. "You did. You just gotta believe it."

Riley walked into an empty house. No pancakes on the counter. No humming in the kitchen. No floral bags on the sink. Just Stace's bags by the door, waiting for her to pick them up in a little while. Soon, she'd be going back to her house for good.

Suddenly the thought of being here when she walked out of his life was too much. Riley headed across the lawn to his grandmother's house. A light burned in the morning room, and through the glass doors, he could see Mary, sitting in the same chair she always sat in, reading a book, with Heidi snoozing at her feet.

He slipped in through the French doors. "Hey, Gran."

Mary looked up and her face brightened. Heidi gave him a quick look then went back to her puppy dreams. "Riley. Come, sit down."

He did as she asked, thinking how odd it was to be back in the same spot as before. But this time, Riley had returned with a new attitude, a new purpose. Stace Kettering had had a lot to do with that. So had the changes he had made in his life. He'd just come from a meeting that had given him a whole new direction. One that sent a charge through him every time he thought about it.

He'd had a lot of time to think while he'd cleaned up from the fundraiser. He'd looked at all the people opening their hearts and homes to a pet. Taking on responsibility, commitment.

And looking happy as hell to do it. When had he last felt that happy?

When he'd nailed a bright blue tarp on Stace Kettering's roof while she watched and worried from below. Working at the diner, side by side with her, learning what a true work ethic was, and finding it was a whole lot more satisfying than he'd expected.

"I wanted to thank you," he said to his grandmother.

"For what?"

"For raising me. For loving me. And most of all, for kicking me out of the nest." He grinned. "I never would have realized what I wanted if you hadn't done that. You were a hundred percent right to do what you did and I appreciate it. That's why I'm going to…quit."

Mary arched a brow. "Quit?"

"I'm not going back to McKenna Media, Gran. I'm sorry. I know you were counting on a McKenna taking over when you retired, but that's not going to be me."

Mary leaned forward, smiling. "I would have loved to have one of my grandsons run the company when I stepped down, but I realize you all need to carve out your own niche in life. I'll promote someone or hire someone. It doesn't matter. What I care about is whether you and your brothers are happy."

Finn was. Brody had found his purpose. That left just Riley. "I'm working on it, Gran."

Worry creased her brow. "What are you going to do now, Riley?"

"Be just fine, Gran. Just fine." He rose out of his chair, gave his grandmother a kiss on the cheek, then headed back outside. To find the one thing he had really come home to find.

The water sluiced over her skin in a gentle caress as Stace made her way from one end of the pool to the other. She swam back and forth, back and forth, letting the laps ease her stress and clear her mind.

She'd come back to Riley's house alone—Jeremy and Lisa had gone out to talk and catch up—and found it empty. She should have grabbed her bags and left, but she couldn't resist one last dip in the pool. Each stroke numbed her thoughts a little more, but she suspected she could swim for a year and still not forget Riley McKenna.

Because she had fallen in love with him. Somewhere between the tarp on her roof and the shelf for her mother's teacups, she had fallen in love, and no matter how much she wished otherwise, she knew she'd never be able to excise him from her heart. Riley had made an indelible impression on her life.

There was a splash from behind her. Stace drew up, and planted her feet on the bottom. She wiped the water out of her eyes and turned to find Riley, standing beside her, still fully dressed—

And soaking wet.

"What are you doing here?" she asked. "In the pool? In your clothes?"

"Stopping you from leaving."

"I wasn't going anywhere yet. I stopped to take a swim." Then she realized this wasn't her property and she didn't have a right to the pool. Not anymore. "I'm sorry, I should have asked first."

"You're fine." He chuckled. "You can swim every day if you want."

"I won't make the journey over here from Dorchester." It was, in fact, the last time she'd ever be in this pool, and a part of her had just wanted to say goodbye. She turned toward the concrete steps. "Let me just get out of here and—"

He hauled her back. She slipped a little and collided with his chest. Riley wrapped an arm around her waist, and righted her again. But he didn't let go. "Stop running, Stace."

"I'm not." She lifted her gaze to his. "Okay, maybe I am."

"You are. Take it from me, the expert. I ran from anything that smacked of responsibility my whole life." He tipped her chin to his. "But no more. I finally found something worth staying for."

"What's that?"

A slow smile curved across his face. "You."

"If you're talking about the diner, I'll hire someone else. It'll be fine."

"I'm not talking about the diner. I know you'll be okay with that. And I think you could hire a monkey who could do a better job than me."

She laughed a little and shook her head. Those damned tears kept burning in the back of her eyes. "I think...you're going to be pretty irreplaceable, Riley."

"Just at the Morning Glory?"

She could have lied. Could have made up something flip. But Stace was tired of keeping her heart under lock and key. "No. For me, too."

The grin widened on Riley's face. "You have no idea how glad I am to hear that." He cupped her chin and let his thumb trace her jaw. "It took me a while, but I finally realized that being responsible, being committed, being dependable, wasn't some evil curse. It was a risk. One I had always been afraid to take. Then I met you, and Jeremy, and everything changed. First it was the lasagna, then it was the pancakes on the counter."

"Pancakes? What pancakes?" The water swirled around them, warm and gentle. The low hum of the filter provided a quiet undertow for their voices.

"The ones you left for Jeremy. I saw those, and I was jealous of a teenage boy whose aunt loved him enough to leave him pancakes in the morning. And I realized that the only way I was going to have pancakes on my counter was to open my heart."

"Is that what you want? For me to cook you breakfast?"

"No. I want to *have* breakfast with you every day. And lunch. And dinner. And go to bed with you and wake up with you." He paused and his blue eyes met hers. "I want to build a house and a future and a family with you, Stace. As soon as possible."

"Riley...I...I don't know what to say." Was he being truthful? Or was this a temporary phase? She wanted to believe him, wanted to take that leap, but a part of her was still screaming Caution.

"You don't have to say anything, Stace. Because I

love you, and if you aren't ready to love me, too, I can wait." He dropped his arms to her waist, and hugged her to him. "You know, I looked up morning glories. They're a hardy flower. They grow fast, twining all over whatever is near them. They're sturdy and dependable, but they're shy, too. They open in the morning, and then they close again at night. They look so delicate, but they're strong as hell inside. Like you, Stace."

She shook her head. "I'm not—"

"You are. You're a waitress from Dorchester who is the strongest woman I have ever met. The only one who has ever made me want to be better than I was before. And the only woman I have ever truly fallen in love with."

Her heart sang, and joy bloomed in her chest. "You... you're in love with me?"

He nodded. "I am so damned in love with you that it's all I think about. I wasn't going out at night to forget you or to date someone else. I was going over to the office at McKenna Media to plan a marketing campaign for that fundraiser that would knock your socks off. I wanted to impress you, because I thought if I did..." He paused and shook his head. "I thought maybe you'd fall in love with me, too."

He'd done all that, just to win her heart. And here she'd been thinking the worst. "You don't need to impress me for me to love you, Riley. You just needed to put a tarp on my roof." She smiled at the memory of him on her roof, drenched and determined. She'd thought her life was falling apart that day, but in truth, it was just beginning to get better. "I think I fell in love with you that day. Or maybe it was the day in the cemetery. Or the day you ballroom danced with me in a hallway. There were a hundred moments when you stole my heart."

"And I'm never giving it back." He leaned down

and kissed her. A simple, sweet kiss this time, one that left her feeling loved and treasured. "I love you, Stace Kettering. And I want to marry you."

Marriage. The biggest risk of all. Binding her life to Riley's, depending on him to be there today, tomorrow, the next day. She thought of the Riley the media had depicted. Then she thought of the Riley she had met, and fallen in love with. The real Riley McKenna was the man who would do anything for the people he loved. She knew that now, to the very core of her being. "I want to marry you, too."

"Really? Oh, Stace." The smile exploded on his face and he hoisted her up to press another kiss to her lips, then lowered her to the water again. "How about we get married at the Morning Glory? I think it's time to build some happy memories in that diner."

This man knew her so well. Knew everything that made her tick. She leaned into him, pressed her head to his heart. "That sounds perfect."

"Good. We'll wait for Frank to come back from Europe. That should give me enough time to settle in at my new job."

"At the marketing agency?"

"Nope. At the Wilmont Academy." Riley grinned, and she could see pride and excitement shimmering in his eyes. "They needed someone to run an after-school program for at-risk kids. I'll be teaching the kids art and woodworking and whatever else gets them to open up and see there are other possibilities in their life than running away."

"That sounds perfect. For the kids, for you." Riley had the perfect personality for a program like that. Approachable, funny, and experienced in life's difficulties.

"Already got my first student. Jeremy." He grinned. "I think I've got a budding carpenter on my hands."

She thought of the days ahead, while all of them adjusted to Lisa's return. Jeremy would undoubtedly have rocky days. "He's going to need that male influence for a while."

"And I'm honored to be that for him."

They climbed out of the pool, hand in hand. Riley wrapped Stace in a towel, then hugged her to him. Warmth flooded her body, though she thought it was more from Riley than the terry cloth. She tilted her chin to kiss him. She loved this man and couldn't wait to see what the future brought for the two of them. Frank had been right—she had found Mr. Right. "Can I ask you something?"

"Anything."

"What was with you and ordering any old thing you wanted at the diner?"

"I did it because I knew what I liked and I wanted it." He trailed a finger down her nose. "Sort of like when I jumped in the pool to go after the woman I liked."

She laughed. "In other words, you're spoiled."

"*Was* spoiled. You have reformed me, Stace Kettering." He grinned. "More or less."

"Me? All I did was give you an apron."

He shook his head and his blue eyes caught hers. In that gaze, she saw love, joy and all the things she had craved in her life but never dared to hope she could have. "You've done a lot more than that. A lot more." Then he leaned down and kissed her and placed the only order either one of them wanted—one meal of forever, with a side of happy ending.

* * * * *

REQUEST YOUR FREE BOOKS!
2 FREE NOVELS PLUS 2 FREE GIFTS!

Harlequin *Romance*

From the Heart, For the Heart

The scandal continues
in The Santina Crown miniseries
with *USA TODAY* bestselling author

Sarah Morgan

Second in line to the throne, Matteo Santina
knows a thing or two about keeping his cool under
pressure. But when pop star singer Izzy Jackson
shows up to her sister's wedding and makes
a scandalous scene that goes against all royal
protocol, Matteo whisks her offstage, into his limo
and straight to his luxury palazzo.... Rumor has it
that they have yet to emerge!

DEFYING THE PRINCE

Available August 21 wherever books are sold!

*Harlequin® Romance author **Barbara Wallace** brings you
a romantic new tale of finding love unexpectedly in*
MR. RIGHT, NEXT DOOR!

Enjoy this sneak-peek excerpt.

"IT'S TOO BEAUTIFUL A DAY to spend stuck inside. Come
with me."

"I can't. I have to work."

"Yes, you can," Grant replied, closing the last couple
of steps between them and tucking a finger underneath her
chin. "You know you want to."

"So, you're a mind reader now?" The response might
have worked better if her jaw weren't quivering from his
touch.

"Not a mind reader," he replied. "Eye reader. And yours
are saying an awful lot."

His touch was making her insides quiver. She wanted
desperately to look away and refuse to make eye contact
with him, but pride wouldn't let her. Instead, she forced
herself to keep her features as bland as possible so he
wouldn't see that a part of her—the very female part—did
want to go with him. It also wanted to feel more of his
touch, and the common sense part of her was having a hard
time forming an opposing argument.

"If so, then no doubt you know they're saying 'remove
your hand.'"

He chuckled. Soft and low. *A bedroom laugh.* "Did you
know they flash when you're being stubborn?"

Rather than argue, Sophie swallowed her pride and
looked to his feet.

"You so don't want me to move my hand, either."

"You're incorrigible. You know that, right?"

"Thank you."

"I still want you to move your hand."

"If you insist…." Suddenly his hands were cupping her cheeks, drawing her parted lips under his. Sophie's gasp was lost in her throat. As she expected, he tasted of peppermint and coffee and…and….

And, oh wow, could he kiss!

It ended and her eyelids fluttered open. Grant's face hovered a breath from hers. Gently, he traced the slope of her nose and smiled.

"Your eyes told me you wanted that, too."

If she had an ounce of working brain matter, Sophie would have turned and stormed out of his apartment then and there. Problem was one, she was trembling and, two, the fact she kissed him back probably wiped out any outrage she'd be trying to convey.

So she did the next best thing. She folded her arms across her chest and presented him with a somewhat flushed but indignant expression. "Do not do that again."

Will Grant convince Sophie to let her guard down long enough to see if he's her MR. RIGHT, NEXT DOOR? Find out in September 2012, from Harlequin® Romance!